P9-BBU-483

LOST in the Backyard

LOST in the Backyard

ALISON HUGHES

ORCA BOOK PUBLISHERS

Copyright © 2015 Alison Hughes

All rights reserved. No part of this publication may be reproduced or transmitted in any form or by any means, electronic or mechanical, including photocopying, recording or by any information storage and retrieval system now known or to be invented, without permission in writing from the publisher.

Library and Archives Canada Cataloguing in Publication

Hughes, Alison, 1966–, author
Lost in the backyard / Alison Hughes.

Issued in print and electronic formats.
ISBN 978-1-4598-0794-5 (pbk.).—ISBN 978-1-4598-0795-2 (pdf).—
ISBN 978-1-4598-0796-9 (epub)

I. Title.
PS8615.U3165L68 2015   jc813'.6   C2014-906673-2
C2014-906674-0

First published in the United States, 2015
Library of Congress Control Number: 2014952060

Summary: When Flynn gets hopelessly lost in the woods, he wishes he had paid more attention in his Outdoor Ed class.

MIX
Paper from
responsible sources
FSC® C016245

Orca Book Publishers is dedicated to preserving the environment and has printed this book on Forest Stewardship Council® certified paper.

Orca Book Publishers gratefully acknowledges the support for its publishing programs provided by the following agencies: the Government of Canada through the Canada Book Fund and the Canada Council for the Arts, and the Province of British Columbia through the BC Arts Council and the Book Publishing Tax Credit.

Cover design by Chantal Gabriell
Cover images by Getty Images, iStock and Depositphotos
Author photo by Barbara Heintzman

ORCA BOOK PUBLISHERS
PO Box 5626, STN. B
VICTORIA, BC CANADA
V8R 6S4

ORCA BOOK PUBLISHERS
PO Box 468
CUSTER, WA USA
98240-0468

www.orcabook.com
Printed and bound in Canada.

18 17 16 15 • 4 3 2 1

For Sam (who brings me on long walks in the woods) and Ben (who wore skimpy little hoodies to the Environmental Ed classes he didn't skip).

I am lying alone in the dark forest, dying.

Well, maybe not actually *dying*-dying. Yet.

I am shivering in a rickety "lean-to" I built out of brittle branches, afraid to move, breathe or even *think* because a huge, snuffling animal I'm too scared to look at seems to be about six feet from my head.

Even though my hood is up and I've stuffed my hoodie with itchy dead leaves, I'm freezing. My Nike Air Force 1 shoes, once a proud and glistening white, are slathered in river mud. This pains me even more than my bloodied hand, throbbing head and swollen eye.

My socks are slimy and very, very wet.

I ate spiderwebs for breakfast.

I haven't slept for days, and my mind is wandering. The cheerful phrase "death and dismemberment" keeps running through my head in a constant loop, and I can't remember exactly why.

Death and dismemberment...death and dismember-ment... Six syllables pounding away rhythmically, like a train on tracks.

Wait. The sounds of the snuffling, snorting animal just stopped. But it's still there. Is it sniffing? Listening?

Time stands still while I hold my breath. My heart is pounding so loudly it seems incredible that the animal can't hear it. Maybe it just did.

The stupid survival books never end this way.

CHAPTER ONE

Warning Signals
(Four Days Earlier)

"Okaaay...and *done*," I said to Cassie as I sent the text. It was a good one. I love texts where you nail it in only a few quick thumb clicks. I wasn't a full-sentence, proper-punctuation-and-grammar kind of texter. I was replying to the stupid, gushy text Nick had sent everyone. Pretty standard Nick stuff: `Oilers game tonite!!! Fifth row tickets dont mean 2 brag LOL!!!` Enough with the happy-happy exclamations, Nick, and oh, yes, you meant to brag.

I just replied, `2-11`. Short and cutting. Nick would understand. The Oilers' record so far: two wins, eleven chokes.

I tucked my phone into my pocket, picked up the papers on the desk and spun around in Cassie's chair.

"Where was I, Owl?" I asked, flipping through the pages idly. "I think we were on the *Death and Dismemberment* section. That one sounded interesting."

"Who are all these people that keep texting you?" asked my little sister, looking over at me. Her room was a mess. Piles of clothes and a huge duffel bag teetered on the bed. A sleeping bag sprawled open on the floor.

"Just…people. Friends. None of your business, actually. Anyway, *did* I read the *Death and Dismemberment* section?"

"*Risk* of death and dismemberment," Cassie muttered, trying for the fourth time to roll the sleeping bag tight enough to fit into the ridiculously small pouch it came in. She was determined to do it right, folding it three times and bunching it tightly as she rolled. Her bushy hair kept falling into her face, and her glasses slid down her little nose. I watched while I swiveled around and around on her chair.

"You need some help with that, Cass?" I asked. I didn't want to embarrass her or anything, but, *man*, just get that sucker in there already. If it were me, I'd have shoved it into a garbage bag a long time ago. Maybe a recycling bag so it looked better. It's not as though she'll get a gold star or a Guides badge if she manages to fit the sleeping bag into its original bag or if it comes out wrinkle-free. Actually, what do I know? Maybe she will.

4

"Help? From who?" Cassie asked.

Ouch.

"Okay, back to the trip disclaimers," I said, scanning the long list. "Because you never answered me about whether I read the *Death and Dismemberment* section—"

"*Risk* of death and dismemberment!"

"—I'm going to read it again. Just so we're clear. Perfectly clear. Blah, blah, blah, *no liability for any and/or all manner of injury or harm whatsoever, including death and dismemberment.* Death and dismemberment!" I said triumphantly, slapping the paper. "Says it right here!"

"You're enjoying yourself, aren't you?" Cassie asked, finally tightening the toggles on the tiny sleeping-bag pouch.

"Sure am! Now how about something a little lighter?" I continued. "Not *quite* so deathly and dismembery." I skimmed through the pages. "Hey, here's one. How about *Inherent, Special or Unusual Risks Associated with the Trip*? That sounds fun! Blah, blah, blah, *slip/trip/fall, bruises, cuts, scrapes.* Wow, here's a long list: *dislocations, concussion, whiplash, contusions* (whatever they are), *sprains, broken bones*...and it ends with *all manner of injuries and/or death which may result from any transportation and/or activity undertaken whatsoever.* Hmmm, that got dark pretty quick there..."

"I'm not as freaked out by a little blood as you are," Cassie said. "Like, from a little cut or something."

"What do you mean 'freaked out'? I'm *fine* with blood."

"Oh, *yeah*, Flynn. You're *great* with blood." She was getting the hang of this sarcasm thing. "You run."

This was uncomfortably near the truth. My family, always sticklers for the truth no matter how awkward it got.

"Oh, *yeah*, I *run*," I said, trying to look vaguely amused and superior. Hey, you have to try.

"Like in that parking lot," Cassie continued, "when you caught your hand in the car door? We practically couldn't *catch* you to put on a bandage—"

"I was stretching my legs! We had been driving, sitting for quite a long time, and—"

"Riiiight," Cassie interrupted.

"All right, all right," I said. "Enough about me. Can we get back to the disclaimers? This is serious stuff here, and we're nowhere near done."

"Mom and Dad have already signed it, you know."

"Exactly. Probably without reading it. Because, seriously? Who would ever sign this if they actually read all this stuff that could go wrong? Leave it up to me to be the adult in the family. Again."

I flipped a page.

"*Insect and/or animal bites and/or lacerations or any and all infections and/or diseases and/or complications caused thereby.* Who *writes* these things? Wait a second. *Loss of limb.* Isn't that sort of like dismemberment? Repetitive. Anyway, I thought you were going on a camping trip, not to a war zone."

"Don't you have something else to do? *Anything* else?" Cassie asked. She was stuffing the duffel bag, which was almost as tall as she was.

"*Weather-related risks such as sunny/hot temperatures (sunburn and/or sunstroke)*...like that's realistic for the end of October...*high winds, rain, fog, snow, thunderstorms, lightning.* Ahh, now that's more like it..."

"Got my rain poncho somewhere," said Cassie. Her voice was muffled because her head was inside the duffel bag. "Yep, here." She held out a dilapidated yellow poncho.

"Rubber boots?" I asked.

"Obviously."

"How about snow wear and/or fog wear and/or lightning wear? C'mon, Owl, you guys are going to be out there in the middle of nowhere—"

"It's only an hour or something away by bus."

"Well, may as well be nowhere, because you'll be in the middle of some dark forest, shivering and wet beside some miserable little sputtering campfire, trying to roast damp marshmallows after some grueling, pointless, slithery hike in the mud." I took a breath. "And that's *before* you spend the night freezing inside your damp sleeping bag on the hard, rocky ground."

I twirled around on Cassie's chair. I thought I had summarized that pretty well.

"Look, Flynn"—Cassie had her hands on her hips, and her face was flushed—"I know you hate camping. We *all* know you hate camping. Probably because you totally suck at it! You don't even try. I mean, who watches YouTube videos all weekend on his phone on a camping trip to Jasper?"

"I was bored. It was boring," I said defensively. "Walking endlessly just to see some lake. Exclaiming over the same trees and mountains for two days. Crouching around a campfire, pretending everything tastes *so good* when it's really charred or undercooked. Getting your socks wet. That's the worst. I hate wet socks. Anyway, it's not only boring. It's also stupid. We have a warm, comfortable house. Why set up a tent, which by the way, is as much protection against wild animals as plastic wrap—"

"You can't enjoy anything that doesn't involve a video or a phone. That's your problem," said Cassie. "*One* of your problems."

How is it that I'm one of the most popular kids in school and my own sister thinks I'm such a loser?

"Uh, thanks for the diagnosis, doc," I said in a withering, sarcastic tone. Didn't even faze her.

"And you know what, Flynn? *I* happen to like camping. I'm really, really excited about this Guides trip."

"Seriously, Cassie—and I swear I'm asking you in all seriousness—*why*?"

She looked at me suspiciously. She probably thought I was setting her up for something. I wasn't, but I felt a little guilty because I sometimes did. Cassie was a good kid. She wasn't cool *at all*; in fact, she was a little weird, and I kind of worried about her starting junior high next year, but she was a good kid.

"If you really want to know, I love nature. It's peaceful. There's no pressure or drama or meanness."

This made me wonder how grade six was really going for her.

"Sometimes when I'm out in the woods camping," she continued, "I think of the earth underneath me and the trees around me and the stars above me and I feel kind of…I don't know, melted into everything. One. With everything."

Cassie's round, serious face broke into a smile. She pushed up her glasses. Then she turned away, embarrassed. "That probably sounds really weird."

"No, no, Cass. It sounds nice. I'm no camper, not *at all*, but I can almost imagine it. Sort of. I kind of get a calm feeling when I play *Skyrim*."

"That's *nothing* like what I'm talking about," she said loudly.

"Okay, sure, it's a video game. But it's set in a forest mostly," I said. "It's very realistic."

I thought about warning her that some people, some grade-six or junior-high kids, might think she *was* a bit weird if she said these kinds of things at school. But I didn't. I didn't want her to change just for other people. She'd figure things out.

I threw the field-trip form on the desk and grabbed the duffel bag.

"Well, I think we're clear about the day after tomorrow's injury and/or death."

"*Risk* of injury and/or death," Cassie said, holding up a little index finger.

I laughed. "C'mon. Let's pack some warm stuff. Do you have enough really, really warm stuff? I mean, *loads* of really, really warm stuff. There was something in those papers about hypothermia."

CHAPTER TWO

Outdoor Education

I thought about Cassie's camping trip the next day as I shivered in a hoodie on the bleak school field. Even though I had clearly chosen several other options (and had even written *Anything but Outdoor Education!* on the option sheet last spring), they'd put me in Outdoor Education. If you have absolutely zero choice, how is that an option? Anyway, I had to endure this lesson in bodily discomfort for a whole year.

Personally, I think it was a money grab: Outdoor Ed cost something like 150 bucks extra for the privilege of endless field trips on smelly school buses to various freezing, barren locales. And, apparently, it would continue all winter, in all kinds of weather, and end in June with the big finale: a three-day camping trip.

I was already planning on skipping the camping trip. I just hadn't figured out how. I was big enough now (almost five foot ten) that my parents probably couldn't physically force me to go. Dad would be disappointed and do the old sad eyes and slow shake of the head. He's a big guy; he could still lift me up and throw me on the bus. But he wouldn't. Dad is the softie, the kind of guy who always helps shovel the driveway even when it is technically my responsibility. Frankly, I was more worried about my mom. She's way smaller than I am, but she would literally pull out the wheelbarrow, no joke. But June was months away. It wasn't even Halloween yet. I had time to bulk up.

But I still had to suffer through Outdoor Ed, which, as the name indicates, was *outdoors*, three times a week. It had been fine, even fun, in September when the weather was good. We took walks in the ravines near the school. We collected leaves, twigs and rocks for classification, which is as useless and boring as it sounds. We practiced building fires, which I thought was pretty brave of our Outdoor Ed teacher, Mr. Sampson, who had twenty-five thirteen-year-olds on his hands. We inflated rafts and "launched" ourselves down the river. We also did absolutely impossible things, like "building bridges" across a stream using only rope.

The bridge-building class was a turning point for me. If there's one thing I really hate, it's wet socks and shoes. Especially *cold* wet socks and shoes. So after rope-burning my hands as well as soaking my shoes while helping to build something that looked more like a drunken spider's giant web than a bridge, I decided to accept my uselessness at everything outdoorsy. I decided to embrace it. I made outdoor ineptitude cool and started attracting a core group of followers. Two rules: one, you had to be conspicuously useless at everything; two, you had to laugh at the try-hards who weren't.

Today, as the wind bit through my white hoodie and my whole body clenched against the cold, it hit me how truly hideous this class was going to get in the winter. It would be unimaginably cold. I hadn't read the syllabus, but I was sure there would be lots of freezing wetness in my future. "Winter Survival Strategies" was our current topic. You would think there would be a DVD about those. One a class could watch indoors.

"This is the kind of day where layers matter!" barked Mr. Sampson. He seemed delighted with the vicious cold and biting wind. He was one of those annoying people who find bad weather invigorating. He probably cheerfully bustles out to shovel at the crack of dawn the morning after it snows rather than burrowing deeper under his duvet and hoping somebody else does it, like most normal people do.

Mr. Sampson looked like a cartoon Boy Scout inflated to adult size. His gray brush cut showed his red ears. His cheeks were pink, and his blue eyes sparkled.

"Layers," he repeated. The class recoiled in alarm as he unzipped his coat and started pulling his shirts out from his waistband. The mere possibility of seeing Sampson flesh had many of us looking at the ground or scuttling to the back of the group.

"See? One, an undershirt, which you tuck in. Two, a long-sleeved shirt. Wool is best. Warm but wicks moisture. Then sweater. Then coat. Toasty warm!" He smiled at the frozen faces in front of him; none of us were dressed in fourteen layers of clothing.

"Of course, any material can act as insulation in a pinch. Newspaper, plastic, grass, leaves, anything! Anything that puts layers between you and the cold. And if your *core* is warm, your extremities are warm." He wiggled his fat, pink fingers.

Why, exactly, Mr. Sampson had to lecture us on clothing in the middle of a freezing field was beyond me.

"See that?" He pointed up to the dark, slate-gray sky. A few of the less miserable, less hunched-over-shivering ones among us peered up. "Cold front moving in! Mark my words and believe you me, it'll snow any day now!"

"Yeah, end of October. No kidding, Sherlock," I murmured, stamping my feet. My friends laughed.

Mr. Sampson went on and on about reading the signs of bad weather in nature, and what to do to prepare for it. I wasn't listening. I felt the same surly, simmering resentment I used to feel when the swimming instructor hauled us out of the pool so we could stand shivering and blue-lipped on the edge while she yakked on about how we could crack our heads if we ran on the slippery deck.

We froze on the field all fourth block, "mapping out" some sort of pointless, imaginary fort that we were going to attempt to build out of snow in future freezing, miserable classes. Actually, my friends and I let the others map while we supervised, which involved huddling, stamping feet, texting, heckling and pointing out errors.

When the bell rang, everyone stumbled frantically on their ice-block legs into the school.

"*My Side of the Mountain*," yelled Mr. Sampson. "You should be finished reading *My Side of the Mountain* for Monday. And get a good start on *Lost in the Barrens*!"

Great. We had to read dismal survival stories about people freezing in the wilderness even when we were in the comfort of our own homes.

When Mom picked me up, I cranked up the heat in the car as far as it would go.

"Hey, hey," she protested, "it's not *that* cold."

"It is if you've been out in the field in the howling wind for an hour and a half," I muttered, fiddling with the controls. "How do you get the heat on feet? Mine are *frozen*."

She looked down at my pure-white Nike Air Force 1s, the coolest shoes on the planet. Birthday-money shoes.

"Well, of course your feet are going to be cold in those. You have perfectly good boots at home."

I let her talk. Nothing I could say would convince her that I would rather be found dead (and dismembered) than wear those clunky Canadian Tire specials she had brought home.

"And a skimpy little hoodie!" she went on. "Seriously, Flynn? It's October 26! You have to start dressing for the weather. Your big coat is hanging right there in the hall. And I bought you that warm tuque-and-gloves set especially for Outdoor Ed."

I read a text and replied furtively.

"Uh-huh, yep, I know, Mom."

"…and you do own heavy *socks*…"

I checked two incoming texts.

"Uh-huh…"

"…so you'll definitely have to wear something heavier when we go visit Joe and Ellen out in the country tomorrow…"

I checked the game scores. And another text.

"Uh-huh…yeah."

I just let her talk.

CHAPTER THREE

Change of Plans

Have you ever wondered how a day might have turned out differently if you changed only one small part of it? I have. Very recently, in fact.

For example, if Dad hadn't offered to help his friend build a deck in the summer, he definitely wouldn't have broken his hand. If Mom had made anything other than creamed tuna for dinner a few nights ago, I wouldn't have made a sarcastic comment about the creamed tuna, which led to an argument about the food, which led to an argument about school/marks/chores. Or if I had walked into the school two seconds later on Friday morning, some *other* sucker would have come in right as Mr. Bruseker was prowling around the corner, looking for help putting out five thousand chairs in the gym for the band concert that night.

But Saturday morning's change of plans was a hall-of-famer. One we would all remember for the rest of our lives.

On the surface, it was an ordinary, everyday thing. It was just Mom organizing everything and everybody, as usual. It seemed like a small annoyance at the time.

Dad read the forecast out of the Saturday paper. "*High two, low minus two, possible flurries.* Starting to get cold."

I looked up from my cereal. "Snow! Are you still going to let Cassie go on her trip?"

He looked surprised. "Of course. They didn't plan a Halloween Howler camping trip at the end of October expecting it to be *warm*. There was a long list of things to bring. She'll be fine."

"Hmm, sounds negligent to me. Aren't parents supposed to *stop* their kids from freezing?"

Mom looked over from where she was reading a book on the couch. She was smallish and roundish, like Cassie. Dad and I got all the height in the family.

"Yeah, we're complete monsters, Flynn. You know she's going to have a ball. She's looking forward to it! So anyway, here's the plan for us: we drop Cassie off at two and head straight out to Joe and Ellen's."

"Joe and Ellen? Our old neighbors? Are you guys going out to their new house?" I asked.

"*We* are *all* going out to their new house, Flynn," Mom said. "I told you yesterday."

"What? When?" I had an uncomfortable flashback to Mom talking and me texting and not listening.

"Yesterday. In the car. After school. You agreed to come, and I've already told them you're coming. So you're coming," she said in the conversation-is-over tone I loved so very much.

"Well, I can't go. I'm going over to Max's house." Everything, *everything*, would have happened differently if I had gone to Max's house. I thought of that later.

Dad looked at Mom's face, sensed an impending argument and jumped in.

"Flynn, Joe and Ellen have known you your whole life. They're disappointed that Cassie can't come, but they're really, really looking forward to seeing you. Hey, they're going to show us the new place they built. Sounds pretty cool. It's totally off the grid—all solar and thermal and whatnot. Self-sufficient."

"Oh, great, trudging around looking at a dirt shack in the middle of nowhere in the freezing cold. *Exactly* how I wanted to spend my Saturday night," I said.

"*So* glad to hear you're looking forward to it, honey," Mom said. I guess I learned my cutting sarcasm from her.

Dad shrugged and let it go. He must get tired of being the referee.

There was no getting out of it. I texted Max.

* * *

At two o'clock I was sitting in the car with the heat jacked up, watching Cassie drag her duffel bag over to a group of other girls waiting by a bus. Mom and Dad were talking with the Guide leader, or chief or president or whatever she calls herself.

Cassie stood beside the group of chatting, laughing girls, looking awkward. She had a woolen hat on that made her look even more like a small owl.

"C'mon, c'mon," I muttered. "Somebody turn around, somebody *talk* to her…" Nobody did. The minutes ticked by as the other girls laughed and shrieked and goofed around and my sister stared at the ground.

Finally I wrenched open the door and jogged over to her. Her face brightened.

"Hey, Flynn!"

"Hey, Owl, just…just thought I'd see if you need anything." My hand closed around a granola bar in my hoodie pocket, a leftover from yesterday's school lunch. "Granola bar for the ride?" I offered.

She shook her head. "No, thanks. I have lots of snacks. Besides, I really hate that kind."

"Yeah, me too. Why does Mom buy these things?" I looked around for a garbage can, then just shoved it into my back pocket.

"Pretty loud group," I whispered to her, rolling my eyes.

"It's okay," she said, looking sideways at the group. "They're really nice."

"Good, good," I said, unconvinced. We stood there in silence for a while, until Mom and Dad came to say goodbye. The girls were starting to get on the bus. Cassie picked up her duffel bag.

"Need some help with that?" I asked.

"It's okay. We're supposed to be able to carry it ourselves," Cassie said, hauling the strap onto her shoulder. She looked at me. "You can *go* now, Flynn," she whispered pointedly. She said it like *I* was embarrassing *her*, which couldn't be true. It's not like I hugged her or anything. Somehow we had gotten to the ages where we only hugged our parents. And even then, only when necessary and absolutely only at home.

"Okay," I said, punching her awkwardly on the shoulder (and I *hate* people who do that). "Have fun. Avoid risking death and/or dismemberment!"

I ran back to the blissful warmth of the car and watched my sister struggle up the steps of the bus and disappear inside.

CHAPTER FOUR

The Drive to the Middle of Nowhere

It was an hour and a half's drive on the highway to Joe and Ellen's off-the-grid house in the middle of nowhere. I watched sports highlights until my phone battery ran out. Dead. Unbelievable. I thought I'd charged it the night before, but obviously not. Bad planning, Flynn, I thought. I had no idea how bad.

I looked out the window at the endless bleak forest of leafless trees whipping by. It went on forever. The sky was sullen and overcast, clouds hanging heavy and low. It felt dark, even though the car clock said it was only 2:20 PM. Why anyone would choose to leave the smooth streets, bright lights and fast-food outlets of the city to camp permanently out here in the wilderness was totally beyond my comprehension.

Looking out the window got so depressing that I actually turned to some schoolwork I had brought along. I read the blurb on the back of *My Side of the Mountain*, the book we were supposed to be reading for Outdoor Ed and which I hadn't even looked at it yet. Apparently, it's about a kid who runs away from New York to live in a mountain wilderness. By himself.

With only a penknife, a ball of cord, an ax, $40 and some flint and steel, he must rely on his ingenuity and on the resources of the land to survive. I sighed. Without even skimming it (which was absolutely all I was going to do anyway), I knew this kid would experience extreme hardship. He would be cold and hungry. But he would also be bravely, unbelievably resilient and resourceful. And by the book's end, he would have tamed a herd of reindeer or a team of bears or something, built himself a log cabin, written his memoir on tree bark with berry juice and cleared hundreds of acres of land to farm in the spring. Something like that.

I could not bear to read it.

"Hey, Mom, Dad," I said, leaning forward between them, "ever hear of a book called *My Side of the Mountain*?"

"I loved that book!" said Dad instantly, swiveling around.

"Hey, hey, eyes on the *road* there, bro," I said.

"That was one of my all-time childhood favorites!" Dad said, smiling at Mom.

I furtively checked the publication date. It really was that old.

"Really?" said Mom. "I mean, I liked that book, but I was more of a *Lost in the Barrens* kind of girl."

This was promising. Two books I was supposed to read; two people who had read them.

"So tell me about them," I said. "I mean, I've practically read both of them for Outdoor Ed, but I want to hear *your* opinions of them."

"Well, both are survival stories, right?" said Mom. "But I guess in one the kid *chooses* to go and live in the wilderness, whereas in the other the two boys somehow get separated from their hunting party up north and have no choice but to survive the winter on their own."

"Exactly," I said, trying to sound knowledgeable. "The kids are out in the wilderness alone. And they survive by doing a whole bunch of things, like..." I trailed off invitingly.

"Well, Sam in *My Side of the Mountain* actually hollows out a tree to live in! Digs and burns out a house from a tree," Dad said. He ran his hand over his short gray hair. "A huge *tree*. I always loved the sound of that. And he makes furniture, and he fishes and hunts. He makes a rabbit-lined deerskin suit. And he actually trains a falcon to hunt for him! A falcon!"

Did I predict this or what? These stories are always so unbelievable. A falcon. Riiiight.

"I seem to remember a lot of hunting in *Lost in the Barrens* too," said Mom. "Our teacher kept pointing out how they used all the parts of the animals, but there sure was a whole lot of killing. Caribou, rabbit, bison. And what was the name of that food...oh, *pemmican*. Berries pounded with meat seemed to be sort of survival cuisine in that book."

"They did other stuff too, right? Those two kids in the *Barrens* book were really creative," I said encouragingly.

"Oh, it's true. Unbelievable what those kids did. They ended up building igloos, storing enough food for the winter and making snowshoes and candles and stuff. The chapter where they fended off a grizzly bear was very exciting."

Was it? Whatever. Why didn't these kids just build a GPS out of wood and twine and get the heck out of there? I found it all highly, highly unbelievable.

"So if you had to compare and contrast the two books or the characters or, really, anything about them..." I invited.

Mom and Dad talked bleak survival stories (making thread from gut! Spearing fish with sharpened sticks! Blocking out wind from a self-built cabin with mud and moss!) while we drank our hot chocolate and ate the donuts from our last stop at the edge of civilization. They talked for a *long* time. I got more than enough information about both books. I felt confident I could discuss them like a pro without actually having to read either one of them.

After hearing that in *My Side of the Mountain* the kid's dad only checks up on him *six months later* (at which time the kid makes a Christmas feast; yeah, that's right—Christmas dinner), I had serious doubts about the book.

And when I heard the author had a daughter she actually named Twig, I refused to read it on principle.

CHAPTER FIVE

Off the Grid

"*Waldeinsamkeit!*" bellowed Joe. He looked around the table at our startled faces. Mom, Dad and I paused, our spoons hovering by our mouths.

"Pardon me, Joe?" asked Dad, carefully setting down his spoon. I could tell Dad wasn't sure if Joe had sneezed or said something requiring a response.

"*Waldeinsamkeit,*" Joe repeated, smiling. "It's a German word my father used to use. And a poem by Emerson. Anyway, there's no similar word in English. *Waldeinsamkeit*: *wald*, meaning 'woods,' and *einsamkeit*, meaning 'solitude,' so it's the special feeling of being alone in the woods. That's exactly how we feel here, isn't it, Mother?"

Ellen (who was Joe's *wife*, not his mother) smiled and nodded.

"Exactly. Being at peace with nature. At one with it."

I definitely needed to remember that word to tell Cassie. Then she'd know she was wasn't weird because she loved nature. Joe and Ellen, some poet and *Germany* all felt the same way she does about being out in the wilderness. And there was a word for it. A word that I already couldn't remember (I'm brutal with languages; just ask my French teacher). But still, a word.

We were sitting in the kitchen of Joe and Ellen's off-the-grid house, which was, thankfully, way nicer than I had imagined. Looking around at the place, I felt kind of ashamed that I'd imagined it as just one step up from a cave. Some dark, dank hovel made of dirt, with grass growing on the roof, a rickety, bug-infested outhouse and some big lever outside that you had to pump until your arm was sore to get a small trickle of freezing, rust-colored water.

I was relieved that this house looked like any other house, with a door and windows and furniture and a bathroom with taps and a sink. It was pretty impressive that Joe and Ellen, who were way older than my parents, had built it themselves. Take that, kids from the survival books. Beats a tree house.

We were eating some kind of hyper-healthy, live-off-the-land vegetarian stew. It tasted like bark and tomatoes, but I was trying to choke down at least a few mouthfuls to be polite. I spread it out over the wide bowl to make it look like I had eaten more and crumbled my piece of flaxseed corn bread into it. The donut and hot chocolate I'd had on the way down here would be my excuse if anybody called me on the food left in my bowl.

Joe and Ellen had always eaten extremely healthily. They were both vegetarians, and they ate foods I had never heard of. Like okra. And kale. The milk they drank was made from soybeans, which sounds supremely disgusting until you actually think about where regular milk comes from. Then soybeans start looking more attractive.

One of the cats wound itself around my legs, purring. I put my hand under the table and stroked Rosie's soft fur. I wondered if I could slip her some of the stew. Better not. I didn't think the cat would eat it.

"What I like is the self-sufficiency," said Ellen. "I like knowing that when the sun shines, we store the energy. In fact, we only ever use a fraction of the energy we store."

She looked over at me. "And Flynn, I have to show you my garden. It's not much to look at now, but it makes the garden I had before look like a postage stamp!"

"Wow," I said, genuinely impressed. "I remember the garden in your old house beside us being *huge*."

"Itty-bitty," said Ellen complacently.

When Cassie and I were little and not so disgusted by eating things with dirt on them, Ellen would give us pea pods straight from her garden. She'd just snap them right off and hand them to us. I still remember splitting them open and marveling at how organized all the peas looked, tucked inside in a neat row. We would scoop them out with our grubby little-kid thumbs and gobble them down, amazed and astounded that these sweet things were the same vegetables we gagged on at dinner.

"So how about water and sewage?" asked Dad, leaning forward across the table.

Mom and Dad were fascinated by this house in off-the-gridland and were asking a lot of questions. This worried me. I didn't want them getting any ideas. Living in the middle of nowhere was fine for Joe and Ellen. They *wanted* to get away from everything; they liked that German feeling of being alone and lonely in the woods. They seemed to enjoy the absolutely eerie silence. Me? It creeped me out. Completely. When there was even a slight lull in the conversation, there was *total silence*. Dead silence.

I'd never realized how much background noise there is in a city. Car noise. Furnace noise. People.

Sirens. Dogs. I reached for my cell phone in my hoodie pocket. It was dead, and even if it weren't, there would be no service out here, but somehow it made me feel better just holding it.

While the adults talked, I looked out the big windows at the backyard. There was a little clearing with a few benches and a fire pit, and then the trees started. A thick wall of trees as far as you could see. A darkening forest on a dark, cold, silent day. Did anybody else find this depressing? Ominous? Apparently not. Mom and Dad were talking and laughing, their faces happy and excited. My spirits sank. I could almost hear them thinking in their clued-out way, "Wouldn't it be a wonderful thing if *our* family lived out in the woods away from all civilization in the middle of nowhere? If *our* family lived off the land? It would be a *great* experience for the kids. They'd *love* it. Kids need fresh air and exercise. Especially Flynn."

I began to ask Joe and Ellen some hard questions, hoping to highlight some drawbacks, problems, hassles and disadvantages of this rustic paradise.

"So, Joe, Ellen, you have any annoying neighbors around here? I mean, uh, out there, beyond the dark forest?" I asked. Why was I talking like I was narrating a fairy tale?

"No, no. No neighbors at all. Pretty isolated," said Joe.

"Ah, *isolated*," I repeated. "Sounds lonely."

"We don't find it lonely. That way leads to the provincial park"—Joe gestured like an air-traffic controller—"that way to the river, and *that* way is forest almost all the way to the city limits. Occasional hunter, and that's it. I love it." Joe was a retired police officer who had probably seen enough of people and their problems.

"Okay, complete and total isolation. Wow. Now how about animals? Bear trouble? Wolves? Other predators?"

"Of course there will be animals, Flynn," Joe said. "Just look around. Forest. It's their home, not ours."

"Exactly! You put it so well. This is *their* home, not ours," I said, shooting a look at Mom and Dad. Mom rolled her eyes at me, which was annoying. I thought I was being subtle.

"Oh, it's been so exciting, Flynn," Ellen said. "Moose! Deer! Right there in the backyard! We haven't seen any wolves or bears or cougars or anything like that yet. But let me tell you, the coyotes can be a nuisance. I don't so much mind the howling, but I have to be pretty careful if the cats are in the garden with me."

"You mean they could get—*eaten*? Wow, dangerous! That's pretty shocking, hey, Mom and Dad?"

"It's just nature, Flynn." Dad shrugged. "That's part of the beauty of it."

Sometimes that man could be incredibly frustrating.

After probing the problems of being snowed in, accessing emergency medical attention, and the lack of a local Starbucks (the last being directed straight at my mom), I gave up.

Everyone was annoyingly determined to look on the bright side of this middle-of-nowhereness, this vast and endless wilderness.

CHAPTER SIX

The Great Outdoors

"So do you want to look around outside?" asked Joe.

I opened my mouth to say "Are you kidding?" but Dad beat me to it.

"You bet we do," he said, gulping the last of his coffee.

Seriously? I looked around at them all. *There's a roaring fire right here, and the idea is that we wander around* outside?

"Yeah, good idea, before it gets dark," said Mom, reaching for her coat. Ellen grabbed a huge hand-knitted sweater.

"You guys go. I'll look after the fire," I said, pulling my chair nearer and stretching my feet out toward the cheerful blaze. No way was I going to wander around outside in the bleak dusk, freezing and pretending to be interested in septic tanks and sump pumps.

"Flynn," Mom said warningly as the others headed for the door, "I think we can take a quick look outside. Joe and Ellen are very proud of this place. And it's *interesting*. Here." She handed me a baby-blue fleece jacket. A woman's jacket. "I knew you wouldn't dress for the weather, so I brought in an old fleece I keep in the car for emergencies. Just put it on under your hoodie."

Mom zipped up her winter coat.

"C'mon, it'll be fun! Let's see what kind of evening Cassie has for her camping trip."

Ellen turned at the door. Her friendly face was creased into an expectant smile.

I sighed and hauled myself out of the comfortable chair by the fire.

Now normally, obviously, I wouldn't be caught dead in my mom's clothes. That goes without saying, I hope. But out here, with nobody to see me, what did I have to lose? My choices were "freezing" and "less freezing." I put on the fleece under my hoodie. It was too small and too short, but whatever. I quickly zipped up my hoodie.

"Okay, okay, I'm coming," I called to Ellen. Then I whispered to Mom, "But can we *go* soon? There's a game on, and it would be nice to catch the last, oh, three minutes of it."

Joe marched us around the perimeter of the house, pointing out obscure little things that made their life at this edge of the world possible. Solar panel this, geothermal that. A lot about being "net zero," whatever that was. I wasn't really listening. But Joe and Ellen were so obviously enthusiastic and, really, were such great people that I tried to mask my desperate boredom.

"Energy efficiency relies mostly on one thing," Joe continued. "Insulation. That was the biggest thing we learned. Extra-thick insulation in the walls, tight seals on triple-glazed windows, southern exposure…"

A whole lot of hassle, I thought, when you could just buy a house on a city street and get heat, Wi-Fi, malls and pizza delivery. I reached for my cell phone, then remembered (again) that it was dead.

We looked at some outdoor furniture Ellen had made out of willow branches.

We were shown some large rocks Joe had hauled in from the forest for a rock garden in the spring.

After we had examined in minute detail the shed they had built and the huge woodpile Joe had "split," we exclaimed over the large, flat, empty patch of dirt that would be Ellen's vegetable garden in the spring.

"…lettuce *there*, then beans, peppers, carrots, tomatoes…" Ellen sketched out the plan of the garden for us, gesturing at imaginary rows. Even while I was literally dying of boredom, I smiled at her enthusiasm.

"And now," Joe said with a laugh, looking like a huge outdoorsman in his padded, checked flannel jacket, "the moment you've all been waiting for. The one, the only, state-of-the-art…septic tank!"

Okay, Joe, I'm out.

I hung back, looking around at the gray forest surrounding the house. It was one of those forests where none of the trees are huge; in fact, all of them seemed to be spindly and tall, but there were about nine billion of them. Mostly leaf trees. Deciduous, I surprised myself by remembering. But there were patches of dark spruce and pine, which were cone-bearing. Coniferous, in fact. My grade-six "Trees" unit was coming in handy. There seemed to be an undergrowth of bushes and a thick carpet of dead leaves. It was bleak but kind of ruggedly beautiful. Mysterious.

"Wow, it looks so much like *Skyrim*," I breathed.

"Or *nature*," Dad said, passing me on his way to view the disgusting plumbing.

I'd had enough of Mom and Dad and this whole thing. I'd done my duty, stumbling around out here on the frozen ground, faking interest in every miserable bush and rock that Joe and Ellen had, for some reason, hauled to the middle of nowhere. I liked them, they were nice people, and they'd done a good job of being pioneer types when they didn't have to be, but *enough*.

I just wanted to be alone. This was unusual for me. Usually, I had a friend over or was over at a friend's or was texting friends or bugging Cassie. But right now, alone seemed to be the best option.

"Hey, guys, I'm just going to go for a little walk in the backyard," I said, gesturing at the forest. Mom was getting on my nerves with her nagging about staying warm and being polite, and the taunting about me being soft and clueless. I would spend a little time out in the forest and show her that I could appreciate nature like anyone else.

"Sure, okay," Dad said, looking pleasantly surprised.

"Hope you find *waldeinsamkeit*, Flynn," called Joe.

Yeah, that was the word. That word for feeling at peace alone in the woods.

Okay, I was up for trying this *walmartkenshdat* thing. I usually had a good feeling playing *Skyrim*. How different could it be?

"Just be a *little* careful, Flynn," called Ellen. "The path peters out after a certain point, and there's a steep—"

"Ellen," interrupted my mom, laughing, "this is *Flynn* we're talking about. *Flynn*. It's cold. It's nature. Believe me, he won't go far. Have fun on your big hike, honey!"

Joe, Ellen, Mom and Dad turned away, laughing and talking, and disappeared around the side of the house.

I stalked straight into the forest.

CHAPTER SEVEN

Alone

I followed the winding path into the trees until I couldn't see the house anymore. It was a relief to get away. I thought I'd walk until the path stopped, like Ellen said, then turn and come back. There was only one path, which Ellen and Joe must have cleared themselves, so there was absolutely no danger of taking a wrong turn.

I walked. It was slightly warmer here in the woods, with the trees blocking the cold wind that had come up since we went outside. I looked around. The forest was completely still. I tried to think about what kind of trees surrounded me. Some were birch—that whitish bark was a dead giveaway. But the others? No clue. Who really cared?

See, that was my big problem with nature: it's boring. Like a museum. Nothing ever happens. You walk, you look at it sitting there, you maybe exclaim at how beautiful it all is (whether you really think that or not) and then you leave. What is the point?

After about ten minutes of walking, I came to the end of the path. It ended pretty suddenly, as if it just got tired and said, "Okay, enough. We're done here." I stood at the end of the path and looked up. The trees were leafless and spiky against the sky. They soared above me, some of their branches meeting overhead.

Okay, I thought, closing my eyes. This is when I should be feeling that *whatchamacallitshmidt*. Peace, oneness with the woods. I breathed in the dead-leafy, earthy, pineconey smells. I opened my eyes and did a full 360. I listened. Underneath the silence I began to hear small sounds. The last of the fall leaves rustling in the wind. A slight creaking of branches. One lone bird. My own breathing.

I felt very alone. Was this a good feeling? A peaceful feeling? A German-word feeling? I didn't think so. It was creepy here. I wondered if there was a ridiculously long and difficult-to-remember German word for the feeling of the forest not really wanting you there, of being in no way one with nature, of being a complete stranger in the woods.

I grabbed my phone to check on this. Oh, yeah. Still dead. I'd look it up later.

I looked around at the bleak, silent, hostile forest.

Whatever, I thought. I tried. We can't all be nature freaks.

I turned to go back down the path. Back to people, a house, a fire. Back inside, where people belonged.

And that's when, in a split second, everything changed.

I heard a sudden rustle and snapping branches very, very close to me. I whirled around.

Something huge and brown crashed through the bushes on my right and charged out of the forest, landing on the path right in front of me in a blur of brown hide and animal smell. It all happened so fast, and it was so loud and so sudden, that I don't even know what it was. Moose? Deer? Something that ate meat? *Cougar*? Anyway, some *wild animal* was within a few feet of me.

I turned and ran. Okay, full disclosure: I gave a muffled shriek, flailed my arms, stumbled into a tree, fell, cracked my knee and leaped back to my feet. And *then* I ran.

I bolted away from the beast, off the path and into the woods. I ran faster than I'd ever run before, even with sharp branches and prickly shrubs tearing at my clothes and smacking me in the face. Terror, I discovered, is a great motivator. Crashing, slipping and sliding, I ran and ran. I stopped once, my heart pounding out of my chest, and listened. Something was still moving through the woods.

I ran again, until all I could hear was my ragged breathing. I was running so frantically that I didn't even see the steep drop into a ravine until I was over the top and crashing down into it.

When Cassie and I were little, we used to roll down a grassy hill near our house. We'd lie down, tuck in our arms and push off. The rolling started slowly and then picked up, until grass and sky all blurred together in an exhilarating whirl and we ended up, sprawling and breathless and triumphant, at the bottom. Then we'd run up the hill to do it again.

This wasn't like that. At all. This was a dirty, painful, out-of-control, thumping, thwacking roll. Sharp tree branches and stumps dug into my legs and back, and prickly bushes stung my face. I gritted my teeth and tried to shield my eyes as the breath got knocked out of me. It seemed to go on and on for hours. Endlessly. It didn't, of course. In fact, if somebody had been there timing it (or, worse, filming it), I probably would have been astonished to find that it had only lasted about thirty-two seconds or something like that. I would have said, "Are you *serious*? Did you *see* that fall? No *way* was that thirty-two seconds!"

Anyway, it was a miracle I didn't get brained or blinded by a tree, because I bounced off plenty of them on my way down. But all hills have bottoms, right? Even steep death ravines in the middle of a forest in the middle of nowhere. I finally reached the bottom a winded, huddled, torn, scratched mess.

"I'm down...I'm stopped...I'm at the bottom... It's over," I muttered to myself.

I lay there groggily waiting for the forest to stop spinning. I was grateful, *so* grateful, for having stopped. I stayed motionless for a while just to appreciate the stillness. I was also afraid. I was afraid that the shooting pains all over my body meant I had sustained all manner of injuries and/or scratches and/or contusions (whatever they are).

Because Cassie was right. I am not good with blood.

I had to have a blood test once, and I almost fainted. Just the *thought* of blood makes me woozy. I can't even watch crime shows on TV. And don't get me started on horror movies. Most people shriek when the main character insists on walking into a dark room to investigate. Me, it's the blood. I can tell myself, "Food dye, food dye, ketchup, ketchup, la la la" all day long, but it always—*always*—makes me completely sick to my stomach.

So I lay there, more afraid of my own blood than of the monster animal, saliva sliding down its huge canines, that might at this very minute be assessing my meal potential from the top of the ravine.

"Stop!" I said out loud. "Stop it!" I said again. I didn't know if I was talking to the animal or to myself.

I looked down at my right hand.

"Okay, right hand, let's start with you. Let's *very* gently…move…each finger…" They moved. The left-hand fingers wiggled too, but I didn't watch them, because when I'd glanced down at my left hand, it was covered with blood.

"Only scratches, probably. Most likely just a scratch or two. Arms? Legs? You ready?"

I tried moving my arms and legs. They moved. Painfully, and not very well, but they moved. This seemed a good sign. I sat up slowly, feeling my head for any gashes or bumps. A big lump on the back of my head seemed to be it. Of course, it's not like I had a mirror. I could feel the scratches all over my face, and one of my eyes was starting to swell.

I looked down at my white hoodie, smeared with dirt and dead leaves, then let my head flop back onto the ground.

Wait—when did it get so dark?

A warning bell went off in my sluggish brain. *I'd better get back to that path. Yeah, that path. That path is very, very important. That path leads to the house that leads to the car that leads to home.* I hauled myself to my aching feet and almost fainted, my head was pounding so hard. Can you get a concussion if you aren't actually playing hockey or football? Probably.

I stood there, swaying. From what I could see, I was at the bottom of a long ravine, the sides sloping sharply up all around me. Trees everywhere, ominous-looking in the gloom.

Where had I fallen? I looked for a swath of broken branches and flattened bushes. There had to be some evidence of my spectacular death-slide to the bottom of this ravine. But there wasn't. There were fallen branches, scraggly bushes, dead leaves and leaning trees everywhere I looked. I hadn't made a dent in the forest at all; it just seemed to have swallowed up my pathetic little trail and settled into calmness again.

I stood still, trying to clear my foggy, shaken-up, possibly concussed brain.

Did I recognize anything? *Anything* that would lead back to the path? *Think, Flynn, think.* I hadn't exactly been taking notes during my rolling fall into the ravine, but did that one bent tree look familiar? I thought it did.

Later I would realize there are a million bent trees that look kind of familiar in the forest. And they're all ones you haven't seen before. But I didn't know that then, and the sight of the tree made me hopeful.

I stumbled toward it, my whole body pulsing with pain.

Out of the gloom a sound broke the silence.

A faraway, thin, *yip-yap* kind of sound.

A dog!

It was a dog barking! There was a dog down here! If there was a dog down here, there would probably be a *person* down here with the dog. If I could just walk toward the dog sounds, the person could direct me out of this forest. A wave of relief washed over me. Things were looking up.

Or so I thought.

The faraway yipping was joined by nearer yapping. A couple of dogs? That seemed odd.

Then came yelping, nearer still.

Then howling. I froze. The hairs on the back of my neck stood up.

Then the whole forest seemed to explode in senseless dog howling. Only they weren't dogs.

They were coyotes.

The coyotes Ellen had told us about. The ones that *stole cats and ate them.* Cat eaters. Meat eaters. I realized with a start that out here in this bleak wilderness, I was not some cool kid in slightly battered Nike Air Force 1s.

I was meat.

I ran.

CHAPTER EIGHT

A Bad Decision

I ran along the bottom of the ravine, slipping, stumbling, reeling, sliding, panting, charging through bushes, crashing into trees. Because it was getting really dark, I ran in a very uncool manner, Frankenstein-like, with my arms straight out in front of me. All to the ferocious accompaniment of howling carnivores.

I thought fondly of the animal that had crashed onto the path. It had been a plant eater; I was almost sure of it. A very, very large plant eater. Why had I panicked *then* when I could have stored up the panic for *now*, when I really needed it?

Coyotes…coyotes, I thought as I ran. What did I know about coyotes? Well, the cat thing, but I was trying to forget that. But if they went for cats, they must hunt cat-sized prey. Or maybe the cats were sort of an appetizer. How big *were* coyotes? Like, dog-sized? What did they even look like? Sort of like mangy wild dogs? *Wild*. That was the scary part of the equation here.

A memory flashed into my mind as I ran. Our living room. Me in a texting marathon, Dad and Cassie looking at a book on the animals of North America.

"*Hey, Wile E. Coyote,*" Dad said, pointing at a picture. "*Used to be the cartoon villain in Bugs Bunny. Pretty hopeless, actually. Always being blown up by dynamite or flattened by a falling anvil. Now these look like much more serious coyotes.*"

"*It's not pronounced kai-OH-tee,*" Cassie said. "*It's KAI-ote. And if you think they look serious*"—she turned a page—"*check out these! Wolves. Way bigger and more dangerous than coyotes. They hunt in packs!*"

Memory is sometimes not a terribly helpful thing. Sure, I now remembered how to pronounce *coyote* properly, but I also had a fresh new worry planted in my brain. Because that flash of memory had gotten me thinking about wolves.

Maybe this mad, yelping, wilderness howling I was hearing came from *wolves*, not coyotes, I thought as I thrashed and twisted through the brush. Wolves were way bigger and more dangerous…and they *hunted*… in *packs*. Packs, meaning more than one or two.

A pack would mean probably four or more, I reasoned. Four or more sets of snapping jaws and sharp teeth. Four—no, wait—at least *sixteen* (and possibly more) sets of sharp claws for the ripping and the tearing…

Suddenly, cat-eating coyotes seemed cute and cuddly in comparison to wolves.

I slithered and pulled myself up the steep slope at the end of the ravine and took off down a hill. The yelping and howling seemed, if anything, closer. Howling is hard to pinpoint. It seems to come from all around you, which is a really wonderful thing to imagine in the middle of the forest at night when you smell of blood.

I veered off to the right, thinking the noise was marginally louder to my left.

I ran until I was completely exhausted. Not just the kind of feeling you get after wind sprints in gym class where you *say* you're exhausted, and Mr. Bruseker, the gym teacher, tells you to suck it up. I had never felt this kind of exhaustion before. My legs were burning so badly they felt like they were on fire. My whole body was aching; my head was throbbing. My *lungs* felt raw (and when had I ever thought about my *lungs* before?).

By the time I came to a little river, I was pretty much just staggering. The howling, a wild, raucous cacophony, was still going on behind me. It sounded even nearer than before. I looked down along the river, which at this point was not much more than a stream of inky black water glistening in the fitful moonlight.

I looked down my side of the bank. Was that a black shape slipping along the bank? Was that *several* black shapes? Or were they shadows?

I froze, sweating and groggy. The wind whipped along the river, and I shivered. I picked up a thick stick by my shoe and turned, facing the shadows. Then I swung around to the river.

Wolves and/or coyotes behind me, possibly slinking along toward me at this very minute.

River in front of me.

Death or dismemberment, or ruined Nikes and wet socks.

No contest.

I lunged into the river.

CHAPTER NINE

Wet Socks

Aaaah! The water was shockingly, unbelievably, numbingly freezing.

My whole body recoiled. It felt as insane as wading into a fire. I forced myself to go on, feeling my way first with the stick. I scrambled up onto a fallen log. It seemed sturdy enough, but you never knew with logs. They roll. All I needed right now was to roll and slip and drown. That really would have been the last kick of a really, really crappy day.

I inched my way carefully along the log, pushing the stick in the water. I tried to reason things out. If the water was up to here on the stick, it would maybe be up to a coyote's chin. Or a wolf's chest.

"You guys can't swim, can you?" I muttered through chattering, gritted teeth. "Not big swimmers, right?

Nah, didn't think so. Seems a shame when the water's so great."

I inched closer and closer to the far bank, until I really thought I had made it.

Then I slipped. I caught myself from doing a sprawling belly flop, but the water engulfed my feet and then my ankles again in a freezing, biting, vise-like grip. I swallowed back the panic rising in my throat. It tasted sort of like Ellen's vegetarian stew.

I staggered the rest of the way across the river without actually submerging my whole body. My freezing hands felt like clubs. My feet and ankles were completely numb. The word *hypothermia* floated through my brain. There had been something in those sheets of Cassie's about hypothermia, some sort of super-serious condition like frostbite that you can get from the cold. Cold water in particular, I thought, but I honestly hadn't been paying much attention. Because it was only supposed to be a *risk* of hypothermia, right? Just the *risk* of it…

By the time I had sloshed and squelched up the bank on the other side of the river, the shadowy shapes on the other bank, if they had ever been there at all, had vanished into the forest. Probably joining the screaming and wailing party, I thought. By this time I had convinced myself that I was going to die, not from being torn apart by carnivorous predators but from the cold water. And dying from a little cold water would be supremely humiliating.

"Nope," I said out loud, panting. "Not dying yet…" I slapped my wooden arms to my sides and stamped my leaden feet. Not much feeling in any of them.

All of a sudden I was mad. I needed those arms and legs for the basketball tryouts coming up. We needed to beat Valley Heights, our main competition this year, and I was the only one who could drain three-pointers semiconsistently. And you definitely couldn't shoot a three-pointer without arms. Or legs, really. Given my predicament, that may have been a stupid or irrelevant thing to think about, but it kept me going.

I found a small clearing on the bank and forced myself to do the basketball defense drill I usually despised. It got us sweating hot in a hurry in a gym. Why wouldn't it warm me up on the bank of a freezing river in the middle of a barren forest?

I crouched low in the dark, bloodied hands by my knees, and moved my feet up and down, faster and faster. It looked nothing like the drill we did in practice, where Coach blew the whistle and pointed and we moved in that direction, our pounding feet sounding like a drum roll on the gym floor. It looked like a bent-over, soggy kid moaning and sobbing and making slow, squelching little steps with his aching, bruised legs in his ruined shoes.

Somewhat warmer, I staggered through the forest, feeling my way with my club hands. I clenched the heavy stick in my frozen right hand. Maybe it was actually frozen to my hand, or my hand was frozen around it. Either way, it made me feel better to have some kind of weapon, though I might optimally have chosen a *Skyrim*-style crossbow.

I soon realized it was so dark I couldn't go any farther. I felt my way around a big tree and slid down, keeping my back to the trunk. At the base, the roots had come away from the ground a bit, and there was a small hollow. I started to dig at the crumbly earth.

Then I heard something scuffle. I wasn't sure where the scuffler was, but I stopped digging and banged on the trunk a couple of times with my stick.

"I need this tree more than you do right now," I said loudly. "I really do. So if you're in there, ready to give me rabies with your vicious little teeth, please, please don't. That's all I need right now. I'm sure you have other trees or burrows or relatives that you can crash with just this one night."

It was a big enough hollow to huddle in, if I didn't mind a knob of root sticking into my back. Believe me, I didn't. I was ready to curl up, and this place seemed at least semiprotected.

I slumped down, shivering uncontrollably.

"It's just shock," I whispered. My mouth was numb, my whole jaw chattering alarmingly. "Shock and cold and freezing wet jeans. It's not hypothermia. It's not rabies…"

I tucked my knees up under my chin and wrapped my throbbing hands around my knees, relieved that it was so dark I didn't have to look at the blood.

"I'll just wait here. Mom and Dad will come to find me. I just have to wait here. I just have to listen for them."

I held on to the thought of Mom and Dad coming to rescue me. Then I thought of Joe and Ellen. Now *they* might be a better bet in the rescue department, being far less clueless and more experienced in forest skills. I started hoping for Joe and Ellen. Then anyone, really. I wasn't feeling picky.

What were they all doing now? Surely they would be worried. Surely they would be looking for me. I must have been gone for hours…

I strained my ears to hear if anyone was calling my name.

I could only hear the yelping on the other side of the river, but it seemed fainter. Maybe the ferocious wolves had sort of run out of conversation. Maybe even coyotes get bored. The more I listened, the more I wondered whether the sounds were actually fainter or whether I was slipping in and out of consciousness.

"Yeah, that's right, wolves and coyotes! You crawl on home. Home to your little…burrows. Dens. Whatever," I called, semideliriously. "See that river? That river is The Line. Your side is there. Mine is here," I ranted. "I may be wet and bloody and hopelessly lost in the backyard, but *this*"—I waved an arm at the forest behind me—"this is *my* side of the forest."

A heroic speech, which I just managed to finish before I fainted.

CHAPTER TEN

Night

I have no idea how long I was out, but I awoke with a start to pitch blackness.

Was that a cry? Was someone calling my name? Was it someone coming to rescue me?

I sat up, cracked my head on the tree root, swore, rubbed my head and listened. Nothing. Silence.

Surely Mom and Dad would yell a few times. Many, many times. They wouldn't yell just once, then shrug their shoulders and head back. Would they?

A terrible, terrible worry had been growing in my head. Would Mom and Dad remember our conversation about those two survival books and actually, conceivably think I'd meant to walk into the forest and live off the land? They would never think that. Would they? Maybe they thought I wanted to be like that kid in *My Side of the Mountain* who left the city to try his hand at surviving in the Catskill Mountains. Maybe they'd come around in a few months, expecting me to make them Christmas dinner, forest-style.

Of course they wouldn't think that. This was me, Flynn. Their son. They knew me. I laughed out loud. But the laugh sounded forced and artificial. And it only started as a laugh: by the end, it was a sob.

It was so dark that I had to put my hand up to my eyes to make sure they were open. My hand was shaking with cold, my whole body shivering. It was incredibly, stupidly cold.

Somehow I had to get through this night without freezing to death.

"Covers, some kind of covers," I muttered, feeling around like there might be a feather duvet or a wool blanket within reach.

I crawled out of my little hole and groped around the base of the tree. A mass of cold dead leaves gave off a dank, earthy smell as I clawed them into a pile. I stuffed them down the arms of my hoodie, then zipped it right up and shoved leaves up the front and back as far as they would go. It actually worked pretty well if I didn't move around too much—I tended to shed leaves at the slightest movement. It vaguely reminded me of a padded Incredible Hulk costume I had when I was five. Only in that costume, I looked jacked and superpowerful. Or so I'd thought when

I was five. In my current outfit, I just looked odd and desperate, but I didn't care.

My legs were a bigger problem. The bottoms of my jeans were freezing into two icy cylinders. I tucked my hands up my sleeves and beat at the bottom of my jeans, trying to thaw or at least soften them.

I groped some more and found a few pine branches at the bottom of a nearby tree. I dragged them over to my little hovel and covered my legs and feet. I curled up again against the tree. It was, admittedly, not perfect. Slightly less comfortable than a feather duvet. But it blocked some of the wind. I was still miserably cold, but not quite as miserably cold as I had been.

I refused to think about any insects that could be on the leaves. Insects? *Don't make me laugh (then sob).* Insects were the least of my worries.

Where *were* Mom and Dad? Seriously, *where were they?* It had to be the middle of the night now. I had an absurd mental picture of them sitting around the fire at Joe and Ellen's, talking and laughing, and then one of them saying, "Wow, 3:00 AM already! We should probably be going. Wait—where's Flynn?" Crazy. Of *course* they had missed me; of *course* they were looking for me. It was just that it was night and absolutely black out here in this lonely forest.

Inky black. In the city, it's never pitch black. There are streetlights, house lights, car headlights. Lights.

And there are always a few people around, no matter how late it is. Some places, like airports, hospitals and McDonald's, even stay open 24/7. But out here, I couldn't even see the moon. Or even one star. It had been a cloudy day, I remembered.

I slumped against the tree with my eyes open. I knew they were open because when I shut them tightly for a while and then opened them again, I could distinguish slight shapes in the gloom. Pitch-black trees against a charcoal sky. I had to stay awake, had to listen for the sounds of the huge rescue operation that was likely under way.

I began to hear distinct noises. The river was a constant background sound, but it seemed to be getting louder. The wind would build up steam, whine and moan, then die down. And you might think trees are silent, but they creak and crack, and they drop cones and branches and leaves. The tree I was sheltering under even vibrated slightly in the wind. This will sound stupid, but for the first time in my life, I actually thought about trees as living things. I mean, I'd always known they were alive, but now I really *felt* them living.

"Hey, tree?" I whispered to the one I was resting my back against. "Thanks. Thanks for letting me hang with you, and being big, and…you know, having my back and everything."

There were other noises. Ones I feared. Animal noises. Scuffling, scurrying noises. Small creatures stupidly bustling and banging around with the sole purpose, it seemed, of waking up predators.

Shut up, you stupid, scurrying things. Do you have some kind of creepy rodent death wish? Do you want to be a midnight snack? Do you? Nothing is so important to do that it can't wait until morning. So just curl up quietly in your hole in the ground or in a tree or something.

I heard an owl hoot and saw a dark shadow take off from a tree and soar noiselessly away. Speaking of sinister night fliers, I wondered if there were bats out here. I tightened my hood.

Once I heard another far-off howling sound. Not the kind of sound that lulls a kid to sleep, let me tell you.

I lay there, red-eyed and alert, teeth clenched and chattering, stiffening in the cold. I jumped at every faint sound. There was no way I was going to sleep. I would stay up all night long. All I had to do was hang on until morning. Everything would be better in the morning. Someone would find me in the morning. If Mom and Dad had given up, surely Joe and Ellen would take a turn, and when they got tired, maybe somebody would alert the authorities.

"Aaoooooowwww…" The far-off coyote or wolf howled again, like that last annoying kid who just will not shut up at a sleepover even though everyone else is ready to sleep.

And that was when I had a feverish thought that made my goose-bumpy skin pucker and get even goose-bumpier: wolf or *werewolf*?

I thought of a movie some of my friends and I had seen last week at a "horror-thon" at Nick's place. We'd all laughed at it then, but right now that werewolf seemed very, very plausible, slinking through the darkness, desperate, so desperate, for the taste of blood…

I whimpered. The trees cracked and moaned and shivered around me.

The taste-of-blood idea made me think of vampires, and vampires made me think of zombies, and zombies made me think of orcs, and orcs made me think of homicidal maniacs in hockey masks, with chain saws…

"Stop it!" I said out loud. I dug my chipped fingernails into my bloody hands. "Just stop it. Get a grip on yourself, Flynn. It's a *forest*. Just a forest. Joe and Ellen *live* out here."

I needed something to occupy my skittering mind. Something that didn't involve monsters and blood. I tried counting backward from a thousand, but I kept losing my place. I went through the times tables, something I'd never done except for marks.

They were remarkably soothing, but once I got up to twelve times twelve, I was pretty much at the limit of what I could remember.

Then I did what I always did at home if I couldn't sleep. It was my own version of counting sheep.

Okay, NHL. *Hockey teams. Western Conference teams.* I closed my eyes and started listing them slowly. *Flames, Oilers, Avalanche, Stars, Kings, the Wild…Predators…Coyotes…*I swallowed nervously and looked around. This was not helping.

Moving right along to the Eastern *Conference: Leafs, Bruins, Sabres, Red Wings…Islanders, Rangers.* I jumped at a loud crack. *Uh…Senators…*There was a quick, light scurrying sound up a nearby tree. *Uh… Senators…*

It was no use. Everything but raw fear (which has a metallic taste, like blood) kept slipping out of my mind as I startled at each new sound.

Finally, I gritted my chattering teeth, stared into the blackness and waited for morning.

CHAPTER ELEVEN

Supplies

It took a few years, but morning finally came.

I started awake from a fitful, shivering half sleep to feel something cold on my face. "Whaaa," I cried, groggily batting at my face with my frozen hands.

My eyes! Something was wrong with my eyes! They were oozing something, there was some sort of crust on them, they weren't opening properly—I couldn't see!

I rubbed them frantically with my bruised and bloodied claws.

It was only snow. A thin film had collected on my lashes and was now melting, the cold water running down my cheeks.

I sort of wheeze-laughed in relief, my heart still hammering painfully hard.

It was snowing in the pale, early dawn, big flakes wafting down and settling like a white blanket over the whole forest. Now that it was light, everything seemed more cheerful. Snow decorated every rock and tree and branch and twig. And every huddling, miserable creature. I stared at the forest that had scared me half out of my wits the night before. It was beautiful, a winter wonderland glinting and sparkling in the fresh snow.

There was a hush, as though the forest were admiring itself.

I broke the silence by groaning as I pushed myself up to a sitting position. Every muscle in every part of my body where there were muscles was aching, and I was so stiff I doubted I would be able to stand up. I rubbed my grimy face with my hands and just sat there, staring stupidly at the falling snow.

I tilted my head back and opened my mouth, and a few flakes settled and melted on my tongue. It tasted wonderful. I needed more. I scrabbled around, scooping snow off a low branch and shoveling it into my mouth. I didn't realize how thirsty I was until I'd inhaled most of the snow in the area. I'm sure an old spiderweb was in there somewhere, because something really stuck on the way down. But the thought of eating a spiderweb for breakfast didn't even really bother me. In my ravenous hunger, I saw it as a little bonus protein.

When had I last eaten? The two gagging mouthfuls of Ellen's veggie stew at about 4:30 yesterday. I was pretty sure that stew would taste a whole lot better right now. *Mmmm, kale, lentils, chickpeas.*

My stomach rumbled. Hunger must be why I felt so faint and weak. I looked around. What did a person eat in the forest? I picked off a little bark from my tree, chewed it and then spit it out. Well, not *that.* It was disgusting, inedible.

Then I remembered the granola bar.

The granola bar I had offered Cassie while she was waiting for the bus. The one she didn't want! *What did I do with that granola bar? Did I throw it out? Is it in the back of the car? Think, Flynn, think…*

I stopped, my mouth gaping open and a blank, frozen look on my face.

Like a movie in slow motion, I saw myself and Cassie near the bus, saw me offer her the granola bar. I heard her say, *I really hate that kind.* And I said, *Yeah, me too. Why does Mom buy these things?* And I watched, still in slow motion, as the hand with the granola bar fell to my side, then tucked the bar into my back pocket.

My back pocket!

I swiveled around on my knees, frantically grabbing at both back pockets. Left one, empty. Right one, something there! I dug it out. It was the granola bar—or at least the tattered remains of a granola bar. A granola bar that had been pummeled and pounded during a huge fall, soaked, then slept on. The wrapper had broken open, and a lot of the bar had disintegrated and fallen out, but about a quarter of it was left. Only it didn't look like a granola bar anymore.

"Okay, Flynn, you don't know how long you're going to be here, so you'd better ration this piece of granola bar. One small bite…" I took a little nibble.

That granola bar was the best thing I'd ever tasted. It amazed me that I would ever have thrown those bars in the garbage when Mom put them in my lunch. It was heaven. I took another nibble. Mmmm. Oats, cranberries, some kind of dry yet sticky substance…

Better stop, better ration—

I wolfed the rest down in one big bite.

Then I licked the remnant of wrapper. Then I dug around in that magic back pocket and picked out the linty crumbs and ate those too. I chewed and gulped that wonderful, soggy mess, wondering again why I'd ever hated the taste of it. I guess when food isn't much of an issue, you get choosy.

The granola bar had gotten my hopes up. I wondered what else I had on me. Maybe I had other supplies. I began rifling through my pockets to see what I had that might be useful. I started with my hoodie.

One dead cell phone.

One gum wrapper. I licked it, then folded it carefully away. You never know when the slight whiff of peppermint might come in handy.

One bus ticket, for when I thought I was going to Max's house.

One crumpled stir stick with my teeth marks on one end.

"Oh, come on!" I said aloud. "Sam from *My Side of the Mountain* gets a ball of twine, a knife, an ax and some flint and steel, whatever you use that for, and this is what I get?" Things seemed very, very unfair at the moment.

My jeans pockets were even worse. Two balls of lint and one small piece of paper with a website for funny animal videos written on it. I stared at the unfamiliar writing. Purple? When did I ever use purple ink? Then it clicked.

"Trust me," Gracie had said, holding the slip of paper out to me, her eyes dancing, "it's *hilarious*." My hand went to my phone automatically. Still dead, of course. And if it weren't, I doubt I would have sat watching hilarious animal videos. I probably would have been shrieking and shouting incoherently at some bewildered 9-1-1 operator.

But still…I folded the paper and put it back in my pocket.

Seriously, that's all I had? These were my supplies?

Wait! Mom's fleece! I was still wearing that hideous baby-blue fleece under my hoodie! I had a knee-weakening thought about how cold I would have been without it during the night. Then, in a flurry of dead leaves, I was unzipping my hoodie and feeling feverishly for the pockets in the old fleece. There were two of them.

The first was empty except for a shred of paper. A fragment of an old grocery list in Mom's writing. *Bananas, cheese, bagels — not sesame seed!* Mom knew I hated sesame seeds. The writing blurred as I read it. I must still have had some excess snow in my eyes.

So anyway, the first pocket was essentially empty.

The second…wasn't. There was a ball of something. I grabbed it. Dollar-store black gloves! Too small, and not food, but they would be warmer than nothing. I would also be able to avoid looking at my bloodied left hand. I gave the pocket one last swoop to make sure there was nothing else there.

There was a little piece of something. I pulled it out. It was half a piece of gum! Gum! I popped it into my mouth almost before I knew for sure what it was.

It took about five minutes of chewing to get the small piece soft, because it must have been about ten years old, but I enjoyed every last minute of it.

Good old Mom. Always tearing her gum in half, saying a whole piece felt too big in her mouth, saving the rest for later. I thought how much this small habit had irritated me in the past, and how much that half-piece of gum meant to me now. I would have to thank her for her obsessive, annoying habit when I saw her.

If I saw her.

I chewed, savoring the faint, decades-old hint of cherry, and thought about my mom. How she could be frustrating. How she could be hilarious. How she was always having friends over or talking on the phone. I thought about how we were kind of similar, and how Dad and Cassie were more alike.

All of a sudden, I felt on the brink of some kind of discovery. I was remembering something from way back in childhood. Something important. Something about being lost. Something Mom had told Cassie and me once when we went into a big shopping mall. What was it? What *was* it?

I had it!

I heard Mom clear as day, saying, *If you ever get lost, stay still. Don't wander. Just stay where you are. And just call for me. Call and I'll find you.*

Stay still. I thought uneasily of the hours I had run and stumbled through the forest. The ravine I had fallen down, and the river I had splashed across. How any trace of that frantic flight was now covered in a layer of snow.

One rule, and I'd blown it. Completely.

"Mom," I said out loud. Then I shouted, "Mom! MOM!" My ragged voice was shockingly loud in the snow-muffled forest.

A couple of birds startled and took flight in a small flurry of noise.

And then the silence of the forest closed around me again.

I staggered to my feet. I had to get back. Just retrace my steps and go back the way I had come. I would have to cross that river again, but I didn't care. It was light now. I would find the river, cross it, climb up the side of the ravine and then be back at the path.

Which way? Which way?

I looked around. There was a bent tree that looked kind of familiar…

CHAPTER TWELVE

Living off the Land

After what seemed like hours of walking in the slushy snow, picking my way around the endless trees, I gave up looking for the river I had crossed the night before.

The sun was high in the sky now and warm on my face. I didn't notice what I should have noticed: which direction it had risen from. I was just glad of the light and the day. But in books, lost people always notice where the sun is. It helps you navigate, apparently. Because everyone knows the sun rises in the west and sets in the east. Or is it the other way around? Sets in the west, rises in the east? No, the sun *rises* in the east (or west?) and *sets* in the west (or east?).

Seriously, I can't even remember probably the most basic fact about the universe here?

Ultimately, it didn't really matter because other than feeling *more* stupid, I had no idea which direction would lead me to civilization. I hadn't paid attention when we drove out of town. Would north lead to pasta, a bath and medical aid? Or south? East? West? Who knew?

Whichever direction it had come from, the sun sure warmed things up. I still dropped into the basketball defense drill periodically, but I wasn't shivering and chattering so much anymore. I had sort of shifted gears and was worrying full time about my left hand, which I had covered with the dollar-store glove. It was throbbing like crazy. I held it against my chest as I walked.

Finally, I decided I had better look at it. Dad, who always shakes me awake from nightmares, says things are often worse in our imaginations than they are in real life. Which was good, because in my imagination, my hand was not a hand—it was more of a claw, missing fingers and dripping with pus and blood…

Stop it. It's probably just slightly injured. Maybe even just a tiny scratch. Probably nothing.

I stopped near a small bank of melting snow and gingerly, gently pulled off my gloves. I started with the right one, because that wasn't the problem hand. Then I pulled off the left one. I glanced down, then quickly away, my stomach lurching.

"Okay, this may be one of those times when reality is worse than imagination," I muttered, my heart pounding. I forced myself to look at it again. My hand was like something out of a horror movie. I almost fainted just looking at it. It was a ruddy brown from all the blood, and there were long black lines, presumably cuts, where the blood seemed to have caked and where some of the glove lint had stuck. I turned my head the other way as I bent slowly toward the snow. Like I was pretending the hand had nothing to do with me.

"Nice and easy...slow and steady. Just going to scrub this hand here—ooh—very, very gently." I allowed my right hand to help but kept my head turned the other way. I peeked sideways. The snow was stained with blood. I looked away. My heart was pounding, and I felt shaky. One hand washed the other with the cold snow until both were numb.

I steeled myself for another peek. A quick one. At least my left hand looked vaguely the same color as my right. But there were still those disturbing black lines...Scratches, probably. Just scratches. Nothing that would seriously affect the three-pointers. Unless it got infected and pus-filled, then started to rot and then...

The hand floated over to where my head was turned away. I peeked again, then looked away. Yes, yes, a definite injury, but nothing some hot water, soap, bandages and serious antibiotics wouldn't fix. I had my right hand slide the black glove back on.

My stomach rumbled. I didn't exactly forget the pain in my hand, but it took a temporary backseat to hunger. I chewed the gum harder. All hint of ancient cherry flavoring was long gone. It was now just a small piece of tasteless old rubber in my mouth. I needed to eat. I carefully extracted the gum, wrapped it in its wrapper and put it in my pocket. I might need it later to chew on or—I didn't know—to set a trap? Build a boat?

I looked around. Food. What did the kids eat in those survival books?

I eyed some clusters of berries on a nearby bush. Would those feed me or kill me? Didn't Mr. Sampson, my Outdoor Ed teacher, lecture us once about berries? I tried hard to remember. It was something about the color. Bright red berries attracting birds? Or was it bright red berries giving the loud "Go away! Poison here!" message? I couldn't remember.

I'd been noticing recently how little attention I've paid to things that might save my life. You know how kids always say "We'll never have to use this in real life?" Well, who knew that that stupid berry class was going to be vital to my survival? Not me, obviously.

I had probably been doing something incredibly important, like texting rude emoticons to friends in other classes.

So back to these berries. In my mind, they had a sweet, delicious, strawberry-like taste. And they were just hanging there…

A fragment of conversation from the car ride to Joe and Ellen's came back to me. Me, bored but determined to get as much out of Mom and Dad as I could so I didn't have to read those two books, asking, *So what did they eat out there in the forest?* And Dad saying, *Well, they looked around at what the* animals *ate, and they tried those things too.* And Mom saying, *Yeah, before they ate the* animals. *There was a lot of killing. Blech.*

Option one! I thought. I pick option one! I liked the sound of eating what the animals ate. Well, I didn't *like* the sound of it, but it sounded like a sensible, blood-free, non-raw-flesh-eating plan.

I found what I thought might be a good lookout behind a couple of large rocks. After doing the quick basketball defense drill to warm up, I sank behind the rocks and stayed still.

I waited.

I watched.

My stomach grumbled again, a long, drawn-out complaint.

Finally a couple of black-and-white birds zipped over to a nearby bush. *Wait — Cassie pointed those out to me last winter.* They were…chuck-, chick-, chuck-somethings. My hand strayed to my phone. Cassie had put a bird-identification app on there that I'd never used. Then I remembered for the nine thousandth time that my phone was dead. But it didn't matter what kind of birds they were. It mattered what they *ate*.

The little birds just sat there, making their neurotic little-bird movements. Tilting the head for no apparent reason. Fluffing up the old wings. Quick, sharp scratching motions with one foot. And then they flew away. Not a peck or a nibble.

No sooner had they flown away than another bird, a guilty-looking little guy, zoomed in and sat on the side of the tree, pecking not at the berries but right at the trunk. *Tock, tock, tock.* This was more like it. A woodpecker of some kind, I decided even without the app. I wondered what woodpeckers actually ate from those trees they bored into. Some kind of sap—perhaps some rich, maple-sugary substance?

Well, in my newfound life of eating what the animals ate, I was willing to give it a try. I found the spot the bird had left, fished the bent stir stick out of my pocket and poked it into the hole. It came out with a bit of gunk on it. I licked it.

Ack! Blech! Disgusting. Putrid. Surely this couldn't be what the little guy had been hammering his head against a tree for. I poked the stick in again.

This time it came out covered in bugs. Which, when you think about it, are almost as gross as raw meat.

I dropped the stir stick into the snow.

Okay, forget the woodpeckers.

I went back behind the boulders to watch for smarter, more discerning animals. Like those other little black-and-white birds.

Chuck-somethings…chuckadillys…chucka…

I thought hard. No. The name didn't start with *chuck*. It started with *chick*. Chick-somethings. Chicka-somethings…Chickabooms, chickaloos…

Got it! I felt triumphant. It was chickadee. The little birds with the cool black heads were chickadees.

Big deal, rumbled my stomach. *So you know what they're called. The important thing is, what do they eat?*

CHAPTER THIRTEEN

So Close

C'mon, c'mon…any time now…

I was still behind the boulders, waiting for some kindly animal to show me the way to the buffet. But I was getting cold. It had started snowing again, and I had just made up my mind to start walking when I glanced over the rocks one last time.

Two deer were picking their way through the forest.

I held my breath. I'd never seen one deer before, let alone two. Cassie would have loved this. I reached for my phone camera before I remembered for the millionth time that the phone was *dead*. So I just kept still and watched them.

They were beautiful. Brown with white markings, long, slender legs, big, sensitive ears. They looked clean and natural in the forest. I thought of my dirt-caked shoes, filthy hoodie and grime-encrusted, barely thawed jeans. How could these deer live out here *permanently* and look so perfect?

One deer, after doing sort of an exploratory scope with his huge ears, began pawing at the snow. The other joined in. They ate, paused and looked around, then ate again. Their heads kept bobbing up, ears alert.

It must be very, very hard to be prey. You'd always have one eye peeled for danger. You could never fully relax. No matter whether you'd just found a great place to stay or some delicious stuff to eat, no matter whether you were drinking or sleeping, you'd always have to be ready to sprint, zero to full tilt, at a split second's warning.

I watched those two beautiful deer and for the first time felt less alone in this huge forest. It wasn't a full-blown feeling of *weinerschnitzelkeit*. I certainly didn't feel at one with the forest or even remotely at peace. I was still freezing and miserable and lost and starving. But somehow I felt better. Calmer.

A crow flew overhead with a harsh cawing sound, and the deer startled, then bounded off quickly, their white tails bobbing. The moment, whatever it was, was over.

I lurched on my stiff legs over to where the deer had been pawing. They appeared to have been eating some kind of moss. I pulled off two bunches, stuffing them into my hoodie pockets. I separated a dirty bit, scrubbed it on the snow and popped it into my mouth.

"Literally living off the land," I muttered as I looked around, chewing the springy mess. It took a lot of chewing. Possibly it was more suited to deer teeth. It tasted like a dirty, grassy sponge. I forced myself to chew and swallow a few bites, then washed it down with a handful of snow. The snow was the best part. Although my hands were freezing and soaking wet in Mom's thin little gloves, I was grateful for the snow. It saved me from having to find some murky, bacteria-infested puddle and consider whether sipping from it would kill me. I'd take the snow any day.

I started trudging through the dense forest, following the deer tracks. They had showed me where a little bit of "food" was. Maybe they would help me get out of here.

As I walked, I wondered what had frightened the deer.

Oh, yeah, the crow.

Then a little voice in my head asked, *But what frightened the crow?*

This was starting to sound like some sort of sick riddle.

I kept turning around every few feet, glancing uneasily over my shoulder. It was probably nothing. Crows were just loudmouths. They always cawed when they flew. No reason. You didn't need an app to tell you that.

I walked on, stopping to do the basketball defense drill from time to time. I lost the trail of the deer in the falling snow and wandered toward fallen or bent trees that seemed familiar.

And then I heard it.

Buh, buh, buh, buh... A faint, rhythmic thumping sound.

I stopped, and the loud shuffling and squelching of my sodden feet stopped with me. I stayed still, listening.

It was a distinctive, machine-like *buh-buh-buh* sound. A helicopter! It had to be a helicopter. I stood still and strained to hear where it was coming from. It was definitely a helicopter, coming this way.

Rescue! I was so relieved I couldn't even think straight.

I started running, looking up frantically, trying to find some kind of clearing where I could wave and be seen. Most of the trees were leafless, but their tops were lined with snow. And the big evergreens blocked out everything else.

I ran back and forth and up and down, skittering in circles, waving up at the tops of the trees. Would anybody in the helicopter see me through all of these trees?

"Here!" I screamed as I ran. "HERE! OVER HERE!"

Bang! I cracked my head on a low-hanging branch. I went sprawling, reeling from the pain. I scrambled to my feet. There was no time to rub my throbbing, possibly bleeding forehead. I looked around and found a couple of pine boughs. I stood and waved them frantically overhead.

"HERE! *HERE!*"

I still couldn't actually see the helicopter, so I kept running, hoping I'd reach a clearing just as it passed overhead.

I did reach a bit of a clearing.

I did see the helicopter, like a huge spiny bird, soaring far over to my right.

It was flying away from me.

I looked around for something, anything, to attract attention, to get it to come back. I squinted against the sun, which was low in the sky, setting in the east (or was it the west?).

Sun! Reflection!

I dropped the pine branches and rooted around in my pockets. I grabbed my dead cell phone in one hand and the shiny gum wrapper in the other, and I held them both over my head, trying to angle the reflection to create some kind of flash. I thought I did make sort of a glint. Maybe somebody looking back from that helicopter would see it.

Maybe…maybe…

Look back…look back…please…please…

"HERE! OVER HERE!" I screamed, my voice hoarse.

I strained upward on my toes, as if those couple of inches were going to make all the difference.

The thrumming of the helicopter died away.

I stood there, waiting, for a long, long time. It might just be turning around. It might come back.

It wasn't.

It didn't.

After all the noise, the silence in the forest was incredible. It was complete, a deadening stillness that lay like a thick quilt over the entire woods.

I looked around. Nothing moved; nothing stirred.

I was alone again.

CHAPTER FOURTEEN

Shelter

I was depressed after the helicopter incident.

Here I was, in the middle of nowhere, in a perfect position to use every swearword that eight years of school had taught me, and I didn't even feel like doing that.

My shoulders slumped in quiet despair. Despair seems a strong word, but it was how I was feeling. I had been so close to being rescued. So *close*. And rescued in such a cool way! Clambering up one of those ropes they let down, soaring above the forest… It would have impressed my family and friends for years to come.

But let's face it: I would have taken any kind of rescue right then. An old guy out for a hike, some backcountry enthusiasts, a Scout group—anything, anyone.

Missing that helicopter almost made me want to give up. It almost made me want to sit right down in my disgusting, dirty, leaf-ridden clothes, close my good eye (the other one was really swollen) and just give up.

I felt bitter. Because, seriously? One quick pass and whoever was in that helicopter just *gave up*? What was it, dinnertime? Pilot's finished his shift at 5:00 PM? Chopper needed for the rush-hour traffic report? The way I saw it, there should have been a whole fleet peppering the area relentlessly until it was dark. And even then, what about those searchlights they use to hunt criminals? *Criminals.* Wasn't I worth that much effort?

What if that helicopter had been my big chance at rescue, and it was over? For the first time since this whole ordeal started, I felt a kind of doom-filled fear. Not just an immediate, coyotes/wolves-howling-their-heads-off, adrenaline kind of fear. A bigger, colder dread. A dread of never being rescued.

What if they couldn't find me? Joe and Ellen's backyard seemed to stretch the whole length of the country. How long could I really survive out here, day after day, night after increasingly freezing night? How long could I survive eating nothing but deer moss?

I felt cold all the way through. Not just the regular cold (and by the way, I wasn't feeling my hands and feet much anymore). This was a desperate, barren coldness that paralyzed me and closed around my heart.

It was one of the worst moments I'd ever had. I stood still and shut my eyes. My mind felt jumpy, panicky, borderline hysterical.

I'll die of exposure.

And if I don't die of exposure, I'll starve to death.

And if I don't starve to death, I'll be eaten by some forest predator...

"Stop it!" I said out loud.

I heard scurrying and opened my eyes to see a large startled rabbit watching me. Probably technically a snow hare, but at the time I just thought, rabbit. He had hunkered down when I called out and was now in a frozen pose. The move-along, just-a-rock-here, ears-back rabbit crouch. But he was watching me.

"Sorry, rabbit," I whispered, watching him back, glad of a distraction.

He was in that in-between stage of brown fur turning white, which must really annoy rabbits. Because the day the snow falls, you need that white fur *immediately* to blend in. To not be a walking advertisement for coyote lunch.

He was so nervous, watching me with his round rabbit eyes. I thought that even if I'd had a *Skyrim*-style crossbow and some conceivable way of making a fire, I couldn't have killed him. I would gum moss and dead leaves and bark before I would do that. He and I were both just a couple of creatures trying to survive out here in this endless forest. He was, admittedly, way better equipped, but still, we were in the same boat.

Somehow, with his roundish body, ruffled fur and serious eyes, he reminded me of my sister, Cassie. Cassie and her group of chattering girls must be somewhere in this huge forest. Wasn't her camp supposed to be an hour away by bus? Which way had they been going? East? West? Once again, I thought hopelessly, I hadn't been paying attention.

Anyway, they were out in *some* forest, presumably surviving. Of course, they had a busload of stuff to help them do it. Cassie would never have gotten herself into this situation, where she was in the middle of a forest with nothing but a hoodie, a dead cell phone and a useless bus ticket. But if she had, and she was here, what would she do?

I could just picture my little sister considering it, owly head on one side, standing there in some lumpy sweater (*mental note: tell Mom, if I ever see her again, to buy Cassie some cooler clothes for junior high*).

"Flynn," said imaginary Cassie in my head, "you're *such* an idiot."

"Thanks, Cass," I said sarcastically. "I would never have known that. But on to the bigger issues here."

"Yes, you do have some immediate problems. What I would do is walk the way that helicopter went and then find some kind of shelter. The sun is close to setting."

"Yeah, yeah, good plan, Cass."

Imaginary Cassie was right. I didn't want to spend another night like the last one. I couldn't. I needed a place to rest, to lie down. I was exhausted, delirious. My head was killing me, and I still didn't want to look at my left hand. The thought of another night out here filled me with terror.

As if on cue, I heard a thin, faraway yelping.

Both the rabbit and I froze for a split second, then leaped into action. He bounded away quickly and easily, a blur of brown and white, melting into the forest with practiced skill.

I dropped to the defense drill to get my body working again. As I thumped away I yelled, "Oh, come on, you guys can do better than that. Any other coyotes like to respond?"

More yelping, closer.

"Yep, second batch. I was expecting you." These coyotes were so predictable.

"Aaaand, almost time for the senseless howling. Who's in for the senseless howling?"

The senseless howling started up. It was last night all over again.

I trudged on in the direction the helicopter had gone, not as swiftly or as gracefully as the rabbit, but he had the advantages of four legs and a fur coat. As I walked, I pressed some snow to my swelling eye. I also gulped down as much snow as I could find. I was pretty sure that dehydration was a bigger problem than hunger, no matter what my stomach was telling me.

I bit all the gum out of the wrapper. I couldn't pry some of it off, so I only had about a quarter of a piece. I chewed it ravenously. You know things are bad when a whole piece of gum that was manufactured in this century seems like an unimaginable luxury.

I started getting nervous, and not only because of the coyotes screaming their heads off. The light was fading already. This is supposed to be a gradual thing, but last night the darkness seemed to settle in very, very fast. The snow had stopped, but it was getting colder. The wind picked up, sobbing and moaning, causing the trees to shiver.

After a while I stopped and looked around.

"Shelter…shelter. If I were shelter, what would I look like?"

I remembered the kid's tree-trunk house in *My Side of the Mountain*. That sounded like a snug place to spend a night in a dark forest. But none of these trees was even remotely big enough for me to fit inside.

Which, of course, made me irritated again that the book was totally unrealistic. Also, the log cabin and accompanying storage shed from *Lost in the Barrens* was out. No time (or tools) for anything like that.

"What do I have here?" I said out loud, trying to think clearly while the coyotes wailed. "What do I have? Oh, would you please *shut up*? Okay, I have lots of trees. I have the occasional rock. Trees…rocks…"

There was one tree that seemed promising. It was a big dead one that was lying on the ground. The base was a big vertical circle of wood and dirt and roots. Growing close to the dead tree was a big evergreen. I figured the pair of them might block the wind from two sides.

I concentrated on a little hollow where the dead tree's roots had pulled away from the ground. Some of the dead roots crumbled in my hands, so I pounded at them with a stick and spread the wood chips out in the hollow.

I scrounged around in the increasing gloom for fallen branches. Most of them were too small for what I had planned, but some were long enough. I put as many long branches over the hollow as I could, balancing them on the base of the dead tree to make the skeleton of a rickety sort of lean-to. Then I collected all the pine and spruce boughs I could find and laid those on top of the bare branches.

I stockpiled rocks on one side of my lean-to. It made me think of a snow fort, where having a pile of snowballs makes you feel better, more in control. In case of animal attack, I could at least throw something. I also found a thick stick that I shoved into my new home.

Then I scrounged under nearby evergreens for anything that wasn't wet with snow—leaves, moss, dead pine needles—and stuffed it into my hoodie. I threw the extra into the lean-to.

It was almost dark by the time I crawled backward into my shelter. It was ridiculously fragile and had already fallen in twice, so I was very, very careful not to touch the branches. It was a pretty tight fit, but the illusion of shelter, the sense of being *hidden*, made me feel more prepared for the night.

My face stung from evergreen-needle scratches. My hurt eye was almost swollen shut, and there was a lump the size of a baseball on my forehead. My hands were clubs, and my feet were useless, numb stumps.

But there was something else I needed to try to do before I passed out.

I was going to start a fire.

CHAPTER FIFTEEN

Warmth

When you're a kid, fire is something you are taught to avoid. You're told to *stay away from those matches, mister*. You're told to walk quickly and in an orderly fashion away from pretend fires in school drills. You have bad dreams about your house catching fire, and not being able to find your family. Even the candles on birthday cakes seem vaguely threatening when lit, and there's always that wave of relief when they've been blown out and the cake is safe to eat. And certain enjoyable campfires I've experienced have turned menacing and sinister when somebody brandishes the odd flaming marshmallow.

But in the winter wilderness, you have to forget all that.

Fire is not only good, it's necessary. Fire means survival.

Only it's not as easy as it looks. Having briefly skimmed two survival books, I knew that lighting a fire without matches, lighter fluid and logs that have dried for years in your garage is a big ordeal.

The smug kid in *My Side of the Mountain* was smart to bring flint and steel (who *does* that?), which I now remembered he used to light a fire. He had to get the hang of it, but apparently when he knocked them together they struck sparks and allowed him to make a fire anytime he chose. The guys in *Lost in the Barrens* seemed to be lighting fires left, right and center. Fire is obviously a central part of winter survival. I had to try.

Paper first. I had Gracie's funny-animal-website note and Mom's old grocery list. Two small pieces of paper. I shredded them into tiny pieces. Then I reached into my hoodie pocket for a little bit of dried moss and a few pine needles I had stashed there. I had a pile of thin sticks at the ready. I'd seen Dad make enough campfires to know you can't start with huge chunks of wood.

Slow and steady, Dad would say, delicately feeding the small flame more paper, covering it with a small pyramid of dry sticks and blowing on it. Dad took a lot of pride in making good, lasting campfires. I used to think this was rather pathetic.

Sorry, Dad. It's not pathetic. It's an actual skill. I wish I had you here now, and not only for the campfire.

I lay on my stomach in my rickety lean-to and methodically made a pyramid of paper, dried moss and dryish twigs. Then I selected two sticks and started rubbing them together. Lightly at first, then harder and harder. I rubbed and rubbed, until I could barely hold the sticks any longer. I stopped, started up again, picked up new sticks, rubbed again and again and again. I rubbed for, oh, about five, six years. Not one spark.

Whoever is responsible for the common belief that you can start a fire by rubbing two sticks together is a complete and total liar. You can't. I couldn't.

My hands were raw, and my head was throbbing in a kind of rhythmic pulse with my left hand. I gathered up the bits of paper and moss and stored them carefully in my pocket. Why? No clue. It just felt better having some possessions.

"Okay, no fire. No big deal," I reassured myself, rubbing my arms. This motion caused a few branches to cave in. "I'm warm enough under here. *Plenty* warm."

I was lying. Even though the snow had stopped, it was bitterly cold. I backed farther into my little lean-to.

CHAPTER SIXTEEN

Wildlife

A sound woke me.

Snuffle, snuffle. Heavy panting and grunting. Big, *big* animal sounds.

I will always and forevermore consider a ringing alarm clock a happy, friendly noise.

The snuffling was close to me. A large animal was sniffing and rummaging on the other side of my tree. Then it slowly circled the tree and lumbered closer. It shuffled and grunted, getting nearer and nearer, until it seemed to be about six feet away.

My hand made the faintest motion toward my cell phone. How stupid. What was I going to do? Video this thing? Text somebody?

No, once and for all, Flynn, you are alone in the middle of this vast, confusing forest.

I lay there frozen with fear, my heart pounding so loudly that I thought it must be audible to the beast panting by my front door.

I wondered if fear has a smell.

Without moving my head, I swiveled my eyes to my evergreen-branch door. It was less dark than the night before, with a clear sky and a shining moon, the slight carpet of snow sending up ghostly reflections.

All I could see was a dark outline that accompanied the terrifying sounds by my head. I couldn't possibly tell what kind of animal it was, and I wasn't feeling in the mood to classify it anyway. It was enough that it was a) big and b) an animal and c) right by my head. It appeared to be digging vigorously, making complicated, jerky movements with its front paws. Then it froze and listened.

My heart thudded. I hardly dared to even breathe.

Suddenly, in a thrashing, snarling lunge, the animal sprang at something, which made a horrible shrieking noise that trailed off to a gurgle. I hoped it wasn't my friend the rabbit.

This tiny episode dashed my hopes that it might be some benign vegetarian pawing for roots and moss beneath the snow by my very head. This was a carnivore for sure, judging by the tearing, smacking

sounds and the smell of…the smell of…oh, my…
blood. The smell of blood! My stomach lurched.

Death and dismemberment, death and dismemberment. The phrase pounded through my mind. Where
had I heard that cheerful little jingle before?

While the animal was preoccupied with its kill,
I tightened my grip on my stick and, as noiselessly as
possible, pulled a few of my stockpiled rocks closer.

I gave myself a sort of pep talk in my mind, trying
to drown out the death-and-dismemberment loop
that pounded relentlessly through my brain.

You are not going to die like this, Flynn!

(*death and dismemberment…death and dismemberment*)

*You're not. Not without a fight. Mom and Dad and
Cassie are not going to find what's left of you beside
what's left of that other dead animal!*

(*death and dismemberment…death and dismemberment*)

No way. If you go, you go out fighting.

The big animal dragged what was left of its kill over
to where it had been digging, right by my tree. It started
up with the snuffling and pawing and digging again.

Closer, closer…

I coiled, every nerve in my body straining.

Closer…

The best defense is a good offense! The phrase came
to me in a flash. I'd thought my basketball coach had

come up with that one, but my dad said it was an old strategy, originally used in war. If you're cornered and sort of sliding into the role of victim, the trick is to turn the tables and attack *first*. Then you have the element of surprise on your side. Also a little bit of control over the situation. And a little bit of control is an attractive thing when faced with almost-certain victimhood.

The best defense is a good offense…

I didn't know how good my offense would be. I had little to fight this animal with. A stick and some stones against its jaws and teeth and claws and demonstrated predatory skills. Not good odds.

But I had the element of surprise. It seemed a small consolation.

Okay, Flynn, I thought over the pounding of my heart, *make it big, make it loud, make it count.*

Here we go…on three…

One…

Two…

I took a deep breath.

Three!

"AAAAAAAAAHHHHHHHHHHHH!!!!!" I screamed.

I crashed the evergreen-branch door back and hurled the biggest rock I had.

I think it connected, because the animal reared back in a staggering lurch. It gave a snarling growl, which was one of the most terrifying things I have ever heard.

"AAAAAAAAAAAHHHHHHHHHHHHHH!" I screamed again.

I threw another rock in the direction of the first, then another. I lunged up from my lean-to and began heaving all the rocks and branches toward the animal, screaming the whole time.

Incredibly, the animal scrambled back, snarling and grunting. In the moonlight, silhouetted against the light snow, it turned and loped away.

Something about how it moved seemed familiar to me. The big roundish shape, the thick legs, the loping run.

Then it came to me. I was seven years old, in the backseat of our car, and we were stopped on the highway into Jasper. Some fool was feeding a big black animal from his car, throwing it pieces of sandwich. My dad unrolled his window and yelled, "Don't feed it, don't feed it," then laid on the horn. And I remember watching that animal rear back, turn and lumber into the forest. I remember how it looked, how it moved.

I stood there shaking like a leaf. My ears strained to hear any sounds.

I may be an idiot. I may be a hopeless camper. I may be lost and clueless without my phone. I may almost be failing Outdoor Ed.

But I had just scared off a bear.

CHAPTER SEVENTEEN

Shelter
(Take Two)

I couldn't stay in that spot.

Nobody could. The hardiest, most experienced camper in the world would be packing it in right about now.

First, the bear might come back. The thought of that made the hair rise on the back of my neck. It made me long for the cute yodeling of the cuddly wolves and coyotes. Second, there was the bear's midnight snack, the dead animal about three feet from my tree. Even if the bear didn't remember it and lumber back even hungrier and angrier, some other forest predator was probably already smelling it.

Time to go. Now.

I grabbed my stick with one hand, a rock with the other, and looked around in the gloom, my heart still pounding. I didn't do any of my usual indecisive waffling about which way to go. I would go the complete and exact opposite of the way the bear had gone, wherever it led me.

I crashed through the forest, slipping and falling and blundering into trees. It was not in any way an organized, well-planned escape, but I kept putting distance between the bear and me, going as fast as I could.

In the silence of that still night forest, I was making a whole lot of noise. Panic noise: panting and thumping and crashing. It began to worry me. I was probably disturbing other predators, who might wake up alarmed and then hungry.

I stopped once or twice, convinced something was following me, but all I could hear was my own raw, gasping breath and pounding heart.

It was exactly like a nightmare. In fact, if you had to pick the setting for a nightmare, that night forest would have been perfect. Eerie, ghostly, illuminated dimly by the thin moon and the snow, the looming, spiky trees pitch black against the deep gloom. The evergreens, the big, fleshy monsters of the night forest, stood like massive giants against the other spindly trees.

I surprised a couple of rabbits sheltering underneath one of these huge evergreens. They shot out, almost giving me a heart attack, and bounded off in different directions.

I stopped uncertainly, straining to hear anything around me. My legs were quaking and burning, and my head was throbbing. I was shaking all over. Fear? Shock? Cold? Hunger? Take your pick. I had to take cover, and if the rabbits thought the underside of that evergreen was a decent night shelter, it was good enough for me.

I pulled my hood tight around my face, steeled myself for the inevitable prickles of the needles and crawled under the low-hanging branches of the big tree. It was so big that there was room to crawl, especially as I got farther in. I slithered as far as I could, right up to the trunk.

I bruised and broke and crushed so many needles that there was a heavy smell of pine in the air. Improbably, here in the middle of nowhere, in flight from almost-certain death, I got the happy whiff of Christmas. And not only that, I found the spot where the rabbits had been. It was still slightly warm from their furry little bodies. It was like a gift.

"Oh, thank you, thank you, rabbits," I whispered. "You are officially my favorite forest creatures."

I lay on my side under the massive evergreen, trying to get my heart rate and breathing under control.

I looked up. What a monster it was, this tree. Massive, thick branches spiraled up above me, wide and black.

I tried to think about nothing other than the tree above me. About how it was shaped like a triangle or a pyramid, its huge branches getting smaller the closer they got to the cone-laden point at the top. I tried to forget that my hand was throbbing and my eye was swollen shut and my face was stinging from all the scratches. I would not think about the bear or the wolves or the coyotes. I would ignore how I was freezing and starving. I would forget about everything except this tree.

I turned on my back in the rabbit bed. It was quiet under the tree, all the forest noises muffled by the snow and the thick branches. For the first time since I had wandered into this forest, I felt safe and protected. I rested my head against the huge, hard trunk.

I glimpsed the sky through a gap in the tree's branches. Unlike the previous night's snow-laden, overcast sky, it was brilliantly clear, stars pricking shining points in a blue-black velvet sheet. I had never learned any of the constellations (I had an app for that, but I'd never used it). I just asked Cassie. Cassie knew a lot of them. She'd call them out like they were old friends.

That's my favorite — Cassiopeia, the queen, she would say, stopping in the middle of the driveway, pointing up and pulling my face over beside hers so I would see what she saw. *See the sideways W? She's sitting on her throne.*

I never saw it and wasn't really interested, but I would always say, *Oh, yeah, I see it now.*

Tonight I craned my neck to find the queen, sitting up there on her throne in the sky. It seemed desperately important to find her. She was the only link out here with Cassie, with home. I hoped Mom and Dad hadn't gone and pulled Cassie from her camping trip. I hoped she was somewhere feeling one with the forest.

I couldn't see that stupid queen. Truthfully, I couldn't see much. Just a small triangle of sky. But one star seemed particularly bright to my eye. I'm not sure if it was the first one I saw, but close enough.

"*Star light, star bright, first star I see tonight, I wish I may, I wish I might, have the wish I wish tonight…*"

I whispered it slowly and carefully, like I was a little child, like it was prayer.

Like it really mattered.

CHAPTER EIGHTEEN

The Way Out

I think I slept. I woke, so I must have slept.

Now if I were one of the kids in the survival books, I would think: Okay, as rescue seems less and less of a possibility, today is the day I plan for the coming winter. I will build a cabin, kill a whole lot of animals with a bow and arrows I make myself and stockpile pemmican.

I tried to think about how I could do any of this without tools or weapons or remembering what pemmican actually was.

My stomach growled.

I pulled some of the deer moss out of my hoodie sleeve and gnawed on that.

Handy to have this insulating eat 'n' go moss, I thought.

I ate the two pieces of paper I'd torn into smaller pieces for my imaginary raging campfire. I ate the gum wrapper. I gnawed and chewed on the string of my hoodie. Not the sort of idle gumming I might have done in class if I was bored. Actual chewing, with teeth and tearing motions. I kept thinking of all the breakfasts I had taken for granted in my life. Just a bowl of cereal now seemed like a feast. Or raisin toast, dripping with butter. Or Mom's *raspberry pancakes.* I chewed harder.

I moved on to imagining lunch and dinner. Pizza, burgers, mashed potatoes, enchiladas…even Dad's "spaghetti squash delite" was looking good right now.

I lay under the tree and listened to the forest. Silent. Still. This silence was getting on my nerves. It was too deep, too lonely.

"Anybody out there?" I yelled. "ANYTHING?" Silence, complete and absolute. Sound just disappeared in the forest, like a stone thrown into a lake. I thought fondly of the coyotes; at least they shook the place up a bit with their nightly howl fests.

I hummed while I chewed on the moss. I sang any song that came into my head, rocking back and forth to try and get warm. It didn't last. The forest just absorbed the tiny sounds; if anything, they made the silence deeper.

I had to come up with a plan. I was dangerously close to staying under this evergreen forever. It was as good a place as any to die. Better, actually, when you considered it was reasonably protected. It would probably not be death or dismemberment by bear or wolf, but just death by starvation.

"Or exposure!" I argued out loud. "Exposure might get me first!" The thought cheered me a little. And, as I was shuddering from the cold morning, death by exposure or hypothermia or whatever seemed like a realistic possibility.

It was the morning of another day. Another long day alone, lost in the forest, with no prospect of rescue. I had no idea what to do. I was so tired and sore and cold and hungry that I couldn't think straight. My thoughts were muddled and confused.

Just give up. A cold little voice cut through the fog in my mind like a knife. *Just give up, Flynn. Just curl up right here and go to sleep. Sleep would feel good now, wouldn't it?*

That cold, dangerous voice scared me almost more than the bear.

"Stop it!" I yelled.

I scrambled out from under the tree into the slush and mud of the forest and stood up quickly. The forest spun in a kaleidoscope of brown and green and white. I leaned down with my hands on my knees until the forest stopped spinning.

"This is nothing, Flynn. A slight touch of concussion, that's all. There. Better."

I gritted my teeth and looked down with my one good eye at my hands on my knees. I took a few deep breaths.

"You will *not* give up. You will keep going. You will hang on. You will find a way out of this."

I ignored the cold, dangerous voice that whispered *How?* and straightened up slowly. I looked around. Which way? Which way?

A flock of Canada geese flew overhead in a loose V-formation, honking loudly, like a rowdy house party in the air. Geese fly south for the winter; I knew that. Everyone knew that. So, assuming these geese weren't as lost and clued out as I was, the direction they were heading must be south. Would south take me anywhere? Would north?

I looked around.

There was a bent tree that looked kind of familiar.

I turned and walked the other way.

CHAPTER NINETEEN

Rambling

Left foot, right foot, left foot, right foot, left—

Stop. Wait a minute.

What was that? Was that a shot? I thought I heard a shot.

I strained to listen, which is a ridiculous thing to do when something has already happened. I guess the point is to listen for whether it happens *again*. It didn't. Already the forest was absorbing the sound, and I couldn't be sure it hadn't just been a falling branch.

Didn't Joe mention hunters when I was at their house several years ago? When is hunting season anyway? Wait, what month is it? What month?

I had a panicky moment where I couldn't remember.

"October!" I said, relief flooding over me. "Of course it's October." I laughed nervously, looking around the way people do when they want somebody to laugh with them. But there was nobody there.

October. Almost Halloween. So when is hunting season? Is it in October?

What if it was a shot? What if there was some trigger-happy maniac out here with a rifle, blasting away at anything that moved?

I stopped, looking around uneasily.

I hope those beautiful deer have cleared right out of here. Gone far away, disappeared into the deep, deep forest, letting it close around them, letting it cover their tracks.

I hope I don't look like a deer...

I'm pretty sure it wasn't a shot.

It was just the forest.

The forest.

Fo-rest, fo-rest, fo-rest.

Left foot, right foot, left foot, right foot...

* * *

It was afternoon, I figured. The sun was high, a white circle behind the clouds. It was cold; the day felt still, heavy and expectant, like it was bracing for snow.

Perfect. I was just thinking that what I could really, really use right now is more snow.

I surprised a couple of birds pecking at some berries. They flew off, and I attacked the tree, ripping off whole fistfuls of berries. I shoved them into my mouth stems and all. They were awful, disgusting, terrible. Sour beyond belief. I chewed and gasped and reached for more and stuffed them into my pockets.

I resumed my sanity-saving strategies as I staggered on. Sour-berry juice dribbled down my chin as I recited out loud, "Seven times *two* is fourteen. Seven times *three* is twenty-one. Seven times *three*… no, *four*. Seven times *four* is twenty-…twenty-four. Seven times…seven times…"

* * *

I seemed to be going slower than ever, so why did walking seem to be getting more tiring? Everything took so much effort. Even staying upright seemed hard.

And a big, gigantic worry was gnawing away at me. I mean, a bigger, more gigantic worry than all the others. There was just no ignoring it anymore: I couldn't feel my hands or my feet. I was stumbling, staggering and lurching rather than walking. I couldn't grip anything properly. My arms and hands hung immobile, like empty jacket sleeves.

I couldn't even remember when I'd last felt my hands—or my feet. This morning? No. Yesterday? When was it?

I peeled off my soggy right glove. My fingers looked swollen and blue. I shoved my glove back on.

I tried to think. I tried to remember.

* * *

Snow was falling. Big flakes wafting down. I stuck out my tongue, tilted back my head and opened my mouth wide. I stood there, gaping stupidly at the sky, hoping for a few more flakes. The cold tingling of the flakes melting on my tongue felt good. It woke me up a bit.

I was sleepy. So sleepy.

* * *

Colder. Sun setting. There was a big tree in front of me. I slid my back down against it and sat in the snow. Sitting in the snow should be cold, but I wasn't cold. I was shivering uncontrollably, but I wasn't cold at all.

I felt hot. I was burning up. I unzipped my hoodie. A pile of leaves and moss fell out and slithered to the ground. I stared at it. *How did that get there?*

Not cold…feel hot…why am I so hot? Probably shouldn't feel hot sitting in the snow.

Then the heat passed, and I didn't feel anything. I felt…nothing.

My body didn't feel like it belonged to me anymore. And that didn't even worry me.

"Tha's okay, tha's okay," I muttered, my head lolling.

* * *

I stared off into nothing, into the dark forest. I was still sitting at the bottom of the tree in the snow.

Dark, very dark.

And then…not so dark. Something happened to make it not so dark.

I lifted my head. There was something there in the trees. Something bright.

Was that a light?

* * *

I stared at the light for quite a long time, confused by it. It stayed there and didn't disappear. It was not in the sky, so it was not the moon.

I didn't understand what it was or what it meant.

Get up, get up! said an urgent voice in my head.

Nah, just stay where you are, my sluggish body responded.

With a desperate lunge, I struggled to my feet. I started walking jerkily, like I was a life-size puppet, like I was on stilts, like I'd never actually walked on my own before. Jerking and staggering, I made my way toward the light.

The light was farther away than I thought, and it seemed to recede the more I walked toward it. But I kept going. I needed to. I don't know how long I moved toward it. Minutes? Hours? I almost gave up, but then there it was: the light was right in front of me.

The light was attached to something.

It was a house.

* * *

It was a house.

Certainly and for sure, that is a house, agreed my foggy, fuzzy brain.

I stood, swaying on my legs, looking at it. It was the back of a house with a porch light that had been turned on.

Click. Another light sprang up a little way from the first one. My head swiveled toward the second light.

One house plus one house equals two houses.

My dull brain did the math automatically, feeling nothing. But I moved forward. Automatically, like a robot that has been switched on. There were fences, but there was also a path between the houses. I bumped along the fence and then wandered unsteadily down the path, my legs nearly buckling. I wasn't making normal connections, even simple ones like *people live in houses* or *I should knock on a door.*

I came to the end of the path and stumbled onto a street.

A street. An actual street out here in the middle of the forest.

If I had been in better shape, I would have recognized it as one of those new subdivisions being built at the edge of town. There were several skeletons of houses under construction, piles of frozen dirt and a few finished houses. I staggered down the middle of the dark street until it turned into another street. There was a streetlight. I stared up at it. Nothing registered.

Two other, different, bigger lights swung toward me in a rush of noise. After days of endless quiet, the sounds were raw and aggressive—emergency sounds. They jolted me slightly out of my stupor, and I flung up an arm to shield my eyes.

The sound of a blaring horn and squealing brakes ripped through the silence of the night.

CHAPTER TWENTY

Just the Ticket

The lights shrieked and hissed to a stop.

Pssshhhhhhhhhhhh.

The bus doors opened.

"Hey, buddy, you want to get killed?" the driver yelled.

"No," I whispered almost inaudibly. "No, I don't."

Oddly, I considered bolting back down the path into the security of the forest. I looked back at it, vast and dense, still and silent. But I didn't move. It wasn't only that it was too far and required too much effort. It was because, even in my confusion, I knew I needed this angry man. I needed to get home.

I scuttled slowly around to the door of the bus.

"Sorry," I slurred. "Just wait—don't leave, don't leave."

I looked helplessly at the two steep steps up into the bus. My legs didn't seem to be working very well, so I grabbed onto the railing first with my hands (but *they* didn't seem to be working too well either) and then with my arms. I managed to pull myself up most of the way and sprawled in front of the driver like a big, gasping fish.

The driver's expression shifted from anger to astonishment to alarm.

"What the—is this some kind of Halloween prank?"

The driver slammed the bus into Park and grabbed his radio.

I saw fear on his face and on the faces of the few passengers on the bus. I looked behind me. What was it? What was everyone afraid of?

"It's okay, it's okay, I'm fine." I struggled to my feet, reassuring them all. Deer moss and clumps of dead leaves fell out of my hoodie as I turned back to the driver.

I suddenly remembered something very, very important.

"Oh, *I* know, I know. Just a sec."

I concentrated hard, clumsily reached into my hoodie pocket and pulled out the bus ticket. It was crumpled and bent and dirty. I unfolded it carefully with both hands, focusing all my attention on getting that ticket into the little slot. The very, very little slot.

"Yeah, dispatch, I think I'm going to need some help here..." The driver eyed me warily.

The stubborn ticket finally dropped, and I staggered backward, shedding leaves and sinking back into the front seat, my arms hanging limply by my sides. I never sit in the seat right by the driver. That seat is usually reserved for those people who really seem to love talking to bus drivers. I always wonder if bus drivers love talking to them. Anyway, that was not actually important at the moment.

"...like an ambulance, police, whatever. It's a kid, and he's in very rough shape..."

"Seek? Are you seek?"

It took me a long time to understand her, but an anxious woman across the aisle asked in a heavy accent if I was sick. Her little daughter was staring straight at me, looking terrified. The woman took off her coat, came across the aisle and tried to cover me with it. It smelled of baby powder and spicy cooking.

"No, no," I said, pushing it back at her, "you'll be cold. I'm burning hot here..."

As the driver conferred with the person on the other end of his line, the mother whispered to her child, holding her on her lap, comforting her. I tried to smile at the little girl to show her everything was fine. It didn't seem to work.

"Hongary? Are you hongary?" the woman asked over the top of her child's head. Still clutching the little girl, she took two crouching steps and tossed a pack of fruit gummies onto my lap before backing quickly away. It was the way you feed strange dogs or wild animals.

I stared down at the fruit gummies.

"Thank you," I whispered. My eyes, for some reason, were swimming in tears.

"Hold on," said the driver, turning to me. "Hey, kid. What's your name? Kid! Wake up! Can you tell me your name? Is your name Flynn?"

"Flynn." I nodded. The nodding hurt, and it started a pounding in my head. I also had trouble pronouncing the "Fl" sound; I pronounced my name something like "Fulynn." I didn't even wonder or care how he knew my name. But I knew this was important.

"'S'right. My name is *Fulynn*," I said as clearly as I could.

The effort completely exhausted me. I closed my eyes. Eye. I closed my good eye. The lights were so bright that they hurt.

The bus was roasting hot. There was so much noise: the driver's excited conversation, the roar of the engine, the little girl fussing, the mother soothing her.

All I wanted was to go to sleep. It took an immense effort to keep my head steady. It fell forward to my chest, I jerked it back, and it fell again. Finally, I couldn't raise it anymore, and I felt myself start to slide to the side.

There was a flurry of noise and movement.

"…he's falling! He's…somebody help…"

"…just grab his legs, let him lie down…"

"…ambulance on its way…here…use my coat…"

"…he's so cold…so cold…"

CHAPTER TWENTY-ONE

Two People

The streets were a blur of lights and noise as the ambulance wound its screaming way to the hospital.

I was strapped to a stretcher, and warm packs burned on my neck, chest and stomach. Everything was too hot, too hot. I kept trying to push back the covers, but someone who had a lot more energy and strength than I did kept covering me up again.

With a clatter, bump and clank, I was shunted quickly, urgently, into the hospital, sliding along the pavement. As we stopped at the emergency desk, my head flopped to one side.

Down a long hallway, I saw two people, one short, one tall. One big, one small. The people looked over and started running toward me in the awkward way adults run when they aren't used to running. The way adults run to catch a bus, bumping and jolting along. The big person ran in a gangly way, all knees and elbows. The little one's bushy hair bounced off her shoulders, and her open coat flapped wildly.

It took me a while, but all at once I recognized those running people. They were Mom and Dad.

They were now close enough that I could see my mom's face.

I wasn't registering much, but I will always remember her face at that moment. It was frantic and fierce and terrified and tender and angry all at once. Dad's anxious, strained face loomed up behind Mom's. Both of them looked white and much older than I remembered. How long had I been away?

The rest is sort of a haze. I know they grabbed me and hugged me, and that it was wonderful and painful.

"Oh, Flynn." For once my mom was at a loss for words.

"Safe, buddy. You're safe. You're home. You'll be all right. Everything's going to be all right." Dad, usually the quieter one, was doing all the talking, gripping my shoulder for emphasis.

Later they told me that before the doctor gave me a needle to knock me out, I seriously alarmed them by babbling feverishly about half-pieces of gum, deer moss, rabbits, pemmican and grocery lists. They tried to soothe me, but I seemed to need to talk.

"Dad, I gotta tell you…gotta tell you…"

"What's up, Flynn?" Dad asked gently.

"I can't do Christmas dinner out in the woods. Nope," I said decisively, shaking my head back and forth on the pillow, "can't do it."

"Okay, okay, we'll just have it at home then," Dad said soothingly, shooting Mom a look that was baffled and alarmed.

"Better that way," I slurred in agreement. "We'll have Ellen's veg…veggie…vegetablarian stew."

"Sure, sure," Dad said. He slipped his hand into mine and held it.

Mom was already holding the other one.

CHAPTER TWENTY-TWO

Home Free

I opened my eyes.

Eye. I opened my good eye. The other seemed willing to open, but stayed swollen shut. My left hand was bandaged and lay on the unfamiliar covers in a useless lump. My right hand had a needle in it with a tube leading to an IV pole.

"Wow. No trees," I murmured, looking around half the hospital room. It was very quiet.

My sister was sitting in the chair by my bed. She turned to me eagerly, shutting her book.

"Hey," Cassie said, pushing her glasses up the bridge of her nose with one finger.

"Hey."

"You okay?"

"Yeah. Just…you know. Weak." Even my raspy voice sounded small.

"Dad's getting food at the cafeteria, and Mom's calling Grandma and Grandpa. I said I'd stay in case you woke up."

"Thanks, Owl."

I thought for a minute. The nickname reminded me of something.

"Hey, I saw an owl out in the woods. They don't make a sound when they fly."

"Really? I've read that, but I've never seen one."

"How was the camping trip?"

"Short," she said ruefully.

"Oh, no, because of me? Did you miss the whole thing?" I felt terrible.

"Yeah. That's okay. We all joined in the search party." She smiled. "It was kind of fun, even though we were looking in the *exact* wrong place. I knew you'd be all right."

"Did you? How? I sure didn't."

Cassie laughed.

Something gave a familiar *brrrrr*. Cassie rolled her eyes. "We charged your stupid, grubby phone. It's been doing that constantly." She peered at the phone on the bedside table. "You have ...216 messages."

She held the phone out to me, but I shook my head. Not yet. And not only because I couldn't feel my thumbs.

"You want to hear this morning's news article about you? You made the front page!"

"Sure," I said. I didn't really care, but she seemed to.

Cassie grabbed the newspaper.

"Front page!" she emphasized, turning the paper so I could see it. "Here goes. The headline is *Find Flynn: Extensive Rescue Operation Called off as Boy Rescues Self*. And now here's the article: *A thirteen-year-old boy is in stable condition after surviving three days of subzero temperatures while lost deep in the backcountry southeast of the city*." Cassie looked over at me. "This is the best part: *'He just wandered out of the forest off Tamarack Point there, right onto the road,' said Dave Wosnicki, the city bus driver who picked up the boy and alerted authorities. 'He looked awful — eye all swollen up, scratched all over, absolutely filthy. Kept shedding leaves every time he moved. The kid staggers onto the bus like a frigging zombie, reaches into his pocket and hands me a ticket!'*"

Cassie laughed. "I love that guy."

"Glad you're enjoying yourself," I said.

"Oh, come on. A 'frigging zombie' handing the bus driver a ticket is hilarious. Anyway…" She continued. "*'This really could have been a serious situation,' said emergency-room doctor Armajit Khan. 'He's a strong, healthy kid, but if he had been exposed another night, his hypothermia would'*—Hmm, you probably don't need to know that…blah, blah, blah…*'We expect him to make a full recovery,'*" Cassie finished triumphantly.

"Yay me," I said weakly.

"Then there's a bit where they interview Mom and Dad. Mom is described as 'tearful,'" Cassie said.

"She'll love that."

"*'It was just a terrible time, knowing he was out there alone in that snow in just a skimpy little hoodie,' said a tearful Helen Davison. 'It was totally out of character for him to wander off like that. Like, you wouldn't* believe *how out of character it was.'* Then she and Dad thank everyone who helped." Cassie looked up. "Tons of people were looking for you, you know."

"Really? Didn't see any of them."

"We were looking in the wrong place. It explains that somewhere…Oh, here: *Falling snow and the peculiar geography of the area impeded the rescue operation, with the boy* idiotically *crossing a slim band of the river that swelled later from upstream runoff. Because it was assumed that the* idiot *boy could not possibly have crossed the river, the rescue effort focused entirely on the areas south and east of the river, while the* idiot *boy made his way north and west.*"

Cassie looked over at me each time she added her own words to the story.

We were interrupted by a nurse bustling in with another warmed-up blanket. After shuddering in freezing wet clothes for a few nights, those blankets were sheer heaven.

"Anyway, that's about it. Oh, they interviewed Mr. Sampson, your Outdoor Ed teacher."

"Oh, great." I groaned.

Cassie nodded gleefully. "Yep. It's at the end…here: *Sampson credits the boy's survival to both smarts and skill. Insulating his jacket with leaves, keeping warm, seeking shelter, conserving energy, hydrating. 'A big focus of our Outdoor Ed program is survival strategies. Somehow, I never thought Flynn was paying attention. But he sure must have been.'*"

"Mmm. I think I've had enough of the news," I mumbled, my eyes closed.

Cassie tossed the paper on the table and sat back in the chair.

"You look pretty rough," she said, tilting her head to one side.

"Thanks a lot." I gave a wheezy half-laugh. "Lots of bruising and/or abrasions?"

"All manner of them," she said. "But there's nothing more serious. Other than the hypothermia, which is 'mild to moderate.' That doctor said that somewhere in there." Cassie nodded at the paper.

"Woo-hoo, no dismemberment! No death!" I pumped my IV fist weakly in the air, the tube flapping against my arm. This small, lame action was absolutely exhausting.

"It was a *risk* of death and dismemberment. Just the *risk* of it."

"Yeah, well, the risk was enough for me."

We lapsed into silence. Then I turned my head slightly and looked at her.

"Hey, remember telling me about how you feel very peaceful in the forest? *One* with the woods? Joe said there's some German word for it, so you're not as freakish as I thought."

She punched my shoulder. I must really have been in rough shape, because that actually hurt.

"So what's the word?"

"Loooong German thing. Starts with *W*." I wrinkled my brow, trying to remember.

"Doesn't matter. Did you ever feel it?" she asked. "When you were out there? Or was it all scary?"

I thought for a minute. I thought of two beautiful deer wandering through the forest in the falling snow, pawing at the ground, quiet and natural in their wilderness home. I thought of the rabbits that had lent me their beds, and that strong, safe, majestic evergreen, and the winking stars in that deep, deep sky.

"I don't know," I said helplessly. "Not one big ta-da moment like you seem to have. But maybe I got bits of it. Bits of it here and there. Sort of squashed between the worry and the terror. Do bits count?"

"Sure," Cassie said. "You know, Mom and Dad said we never have to go camping again *ever* if you don't want to." She added quickly, "And that's fine with me."

I was getting tired again. So tired.

"No, we'll go. Of course we'll go camping again," I said. "I think there were three YouTube videos I didn't watch last time…"

Cassie laughed, and then she looked anxiously at me.

"You look super tired again, Flynn. Like, zombie tired. Better sleep. Don't worry about anything. You'll be home soon. The doctor said you're out of the woods, no pun intended."

She leaned over me and gave me a quick hug.

I was too tired to even move my club hands to hug her back.

"Love you, Owl," I slurred.

"Me too," she whispered, her voice muffled in my shoulder.

I closed my eye, drifting, slipping into sleep.

Out of the woods…out of the woods…

Acknowledgments

Thanks to the wonderful staff at Orca Book Publishers, in particular my editor, Sarah "Hippie-Chick" Harvey, who is a complete delight to work with, even while axing every last adverb, and Chantal Gabriell, who designed the beautiful and atmospheric cover art. Thanks also to Mitchell (who listens to my story ideas) and to Kate (who tells me hers). I would also like to acknowledge Farley Mowat's classic novel *Lost in the Barrens*, whose skilled, hardy and resilient characters don't entirely deserve Flynn's eye-rolling skepticism. He's just jealous.

Alison Hughes is an award-winning writer who has lived, worked and studied in Canada, England and Australia. Her previous books include *Poser* and *On a Scale from Idiot to Complete Jerk*. She read lots of survival stories as a child and used to make elaborate and thrilling plans to weather a natural disaster which, sadly, never materialized. Alison lives with her family in Edmonton, Alberta, where she still delights in blizzards and power outages and tends to stockpile canned goods.